D0058191

# YOU
## ARE THE
## EVERY
## THING

Also by Karen Rivers

ALL THAT WAS

BEFORE WE GO EXTINCT

WHAT IS REAL

# YOU ARE THE EVERY THING

## KAREN RIVERS

Algonquin 2018

Published by Algonquin Young Readers
an imprint of Algonquin Books of Chapel Hill
Post Office Box 2225
Chapel Hill, North Carolina 27515-2225

a division of Workman Publishing
225 Varick Street
New York, New York 10014

Printed in the United States of America.
Published simultaneously in Canada by Thomas Allen & Son Limited.
Design by Carla Weise.

Library of Congress Cataloging-in-Publication Data

Names: Rivers, Karen, 1970- author.
Title: You are the everything / Karen Rivers.
Description: First edition. | Chapel Hill, North Carolina : Algonquin
  Young Readers, 2018. | Summary: When sixteen-year-old Elyse
  Schmidt and her crush, Josh Harris, are the sole survivors of a
  plane crash, she believes that everything is perfect and their love
  story is meant to be, but she finds that fate is not always what you
  expect it to be.
Identifiers: LCCN 2018011476 | ISBN 9781616208158 (hardcover :
  alk. paper)
Subjects: | CYAC: Love—Fiction. | Fate and fatalism—Fiction. |
  Aircraft accidents—Fiction. | Survival—Fiction. | Interpersonal
  relations—Fiction.
Classification: LCC PZ7.R5224 Yo 2018 | DDC [Fic]—dc23
LC record available at https://lccn.loc.gov/2018011476

10 9 8 7 6 5 4 3 2 1
First Edition

For Krestyna,
because there is
magic in the editing.

part **one**

# 1.

You are on a plane.

The plane is an Airbus. You don't know anything about planes but if you were going to draw an "Airbus" it would be more like the regular school bus, but with wings jutting out the sides. This is *definitely* not that. The seats are upholstered in blue-and-black fabric that looks new. There is a tiny screen attached to the back of the chair in front of you that shows where the Airbus is currently flying. It's a movie, starring you! (Or at least, your plane.) A tiny dashed line is superimposed over a map, illustrating where you have been and where you are going. You wish so badly that you could fast-forward along that path until you are home.

You are so totally over this already.

Your best friend, Kath, is sitting in the seat in front of you. Her hair occasionally pops into your line of vision. Kath never sits still. You can hear the tinny treble of the music she's listening to at full volume, even though the movie she's watching is something unrelated. On her screen, two British people start kissing. One of the people is Benedict Cumberbatch. He's your movie-star crush so you change the channel on your screen so you can watch it, too, with no sound. You don't need the sound. You've watched that movie before (eight times) with Kath, lying on her bed, throwing popcorn into each other's mouths—or more accurately into each other's hair. It feels like forever ago.

That was *before* Paris.

You wish you could go back to that, to undo Paris, to undo everything, especially the stupid fight you're in with Kath. But you can't.

Now you can *feel* her dancing, her chair back vibrating your table. She occasionally bumps the person next to her, who is named Max, but it's the wrong Max, not the Max she *likes*. This Max is the one with the ears that stick out, a huge collection of Star Wars stickers on his tuba case, and a nervous stutter: the *Other* Max. The Other Max would never have the nerve to tell someone as tall and pretty and powerful as Kath to stop dancing. The girl sitting in front of her has no reservations about it, though. She keeps kneeling up on her seat, turning around, and glowering. She is pretty and English with an angular face and a loud voice. "Stop kicking my seat, for the love of God," she says. "I've asked twenty times. I need to sleep."

Kath is either ignoring her or rolling her eyes. You can't tell from behind Kath's seat, but you're pretty sure she flips her off.

"Americans have no class," the girl says sharply, not winning any friends on a flight filled with Americans.

"England sucks!" someone yells.

"HEY," shouts Mr. Appleby.

Kath isn't sitting next to you because of the fight. "I'm not talking to you," she'd said. "It's over between us." You couldn't tell from her tone if she was half-joking or all-serious. Then she swapped seats with Josh Harris, which is a pretty huge favor to you, actually. You're really grateful. But you still glare at the place where her head moves to the beat, oblivious to how mad you are. She is in an anger sandwich, effectively, with you and the English girl both furious with her for different reasons.

Josh Harris is asleep. He is making a gentle breathing sound that you wish you could record to play back whenever you feel stressed or anxious. He even *breathes* better than most people.

You change your screen back to the map and trace the plane's path with your finger but before you can get to California, the screen interrupts itself with an ad for car rentals. *Rude*, you think, flipping it back to Benedict Cumberbatch. He's leaning against a wall, laughing. He's putting a toothpick between his teeth. Kath doesn't understand why you find him attractive when he's so ordinary. "Small eyes," she says. "Pinched mouth." But it's his ordinariness that makes him attractive. Anyway, he's number two. Josh Harris is, and

5

always will be, number one. You sneak another glance at him, at his perfectly straight nose, and at his ear, which is sporting a diamond stud. The plane lurches.

*Flying is a suspension of disbelief*, your dad said before you boarded to leave home. Now you know what he means. How does the plane stay up? It's ridiculous. Nothing makes sense.

You lean your head back on the headrest and try not to think about lice. The engine noise is louder than you remember from the flight over, but you were too excited and nervous that time to properly pay attention. Or maybe this time, because you are in the very last row with your back pressed up against the end of the plane with no way to tip your chair back, it just sounds different. Anyway, right now, everything is too loud: the roar of the engine and the voices of your classmates and the other passengers and the way Mr. Appleby keeps standing up and saying, "HEY," and then sitting back down again, as though his work is done. No one is quieter after one of his HEYs, which are completely ineffectual, except in getting the passengers who aren't in the band to look at him and then sigh, annoyed.

It's the return half of your first plane trip, first time out of the country, first time for a lot of things, but *nothing* happened, except the fight with Kath, which sucks. Paris should've been the backdrop for so many amazing things, but it wasn't. You did *not* get kissed for the first time or get Josh Harris to fall in love with you or even have any experiences that forced you and Josh Harris together, alone, where he'd have to notice you and realize how much he liked you. You'd imagined it *so* clearly—you even drew it—that when it didn't happen, you felt ripped off, like somehow your comic should have created that perfect moment. And it didn't.

You'd drawn an earthquake. (Earthquakes do happen in France, after all, just not as frequently as in California.) You and Josh would be trapped in a safe but cut-off room for hours and hours, ideally with some wine and French bread. He'd slowly get to know you, then somehow there would be a bed and you'd fall back onto it, kissing. And all you'd have to survive on would be canned goods. Did they even have something as unsophisticated as ravioli in Paris? You drew some tiny tins, labeled LE RAVIOLI and LA SPAGHETTIOS.

Your next idea was an elevator breaking down, one of those tiny Parisian cage ones you've seen in movies, forcing you next to each other to wait for rescue. Driven together by fate and circumstance! Just you and Josh Harris, waiting endless hours alone together, surviving on breath mints and water, which you always carried in your bag, just in case.

All the comics ended with you and Josh Harris kissing. You never really went further than that, to *after*. To what would happen next. To *more*.

"There's more to being in love with someone than just kissing," Kath had pointed out. "*Kissing* is not a relationship. Boy, are you ever going to be shocked by the real thing one day."

"Like you're an expert," you'd said. "Because you dated Charlie Martin for ten minutes?"

"Well, duh," she'd said.

In reality, it didn't matter what she said, because you weren't *in* a relationship with Josh Harris, or anyone else for that matter. For most of the trip, Josh Harris hung out with Fitzy and all of those loud boys, same as at home, running down Paris sidewalks as though they were in the gym at the Y, high-fiving and generally being oblivious to you, Elyse Schmidt, staring moonily after him.

"Stop staring at him so *moonily*," Kath had said. "Either talk to him or don't, but all the mooning about it is doing me in. I *hate* mooning."

"*You* don't have to moon about it," you'd pointed out.

"But I kind of do," she'd said. "Your mooning is sucking me in. It's like falling into a tar pit. I'm practically fossilized from all your mooning for Josh."

"Josh *Harris*," you'd corrected her. "All-one-word."

"Whatever," she'd said, and rolled her eyes. "I love you, but you're a nut. Also, you're ruining Paris."

If you had to search for something nice to say about Paris, you'd say that the bread was totally up to your expectations: crusty and soft and perfect. A-plus for the bread, Paris! Way to go! Nice work on the carbs! And the river was pretty. The bridges that crisscrossed it were like a romantic movie come to life, especially at night when the lights came on.

A romantic movie featuring zero romance for you specifically, that is.

But the damp cool February air had crawled into your bones as you walked down the Champs-Élysées, and you ached like the old person that you sort of are inside. You've had arthritis ever since you can remember. "Junior Idiopathic Arthritis." Or, as you prefer to think of it, "Junky Idiotic Arthritis." Your fingers ache now, just thinking about it. You want to get home to stick them in the paraffin bath, the warm heat sinking into your joints like a series of tiny gentle hugs, the pain slowly seeping away.

Not only was it damp in Paris, but everything stank: humidity and yeast and dog poop and all those clammy stone buildings. You missed the orchards at home, the peach trees undulating into the distance under the always-blue California skies, even though in reality, you're sick of end-less summer and living way out of town on the farm, which your mom hates (your parents are constantly arguing about it), and the way that peaches are a part of every meal. You suspect that deep down inside, you're not a California person. A California person is all white teeth and easy smiles and highlighted blond hair and perkiness. You're *definitely* not a peach person, which is all that, along with a sweetness that you 100 percent lack.

You're a snow person.

You're a person who has moods, who needs sharp, extreme seasons.

You're sort of a sour person, if you're being honest. More like a bitter cherry than a ripe peach, in any event. When you're mad, you're lightning or an ice storm, wrapping every-thing around you in a frigid, glassy blanket of electric fury.

You write *WYOMING* on your sketchbook and then draw a heart around it, and then some trees. You add a starry night sky. A rolling field. A white horse galloping by. A mountain.

You exhale. If you had seasons, real seasons, and mountains and biting blackflies and cold streams and a real autumn, replete with rustling colorful leaves, then—and only then—would you be yourself. You don't know *why*. It's just the way it is. You just *know*.

*One day*, you think. *One day*.

The streets in Paris were not for you. They were too narrow and too tense and packed too full of shops and doorways and endless people, so many people, people everywhere. It made you feel trapped, closed in, suffocated. It made you miss the sky.

On your first day there, you bought a turquoise blue silk scarf with a pattern of peaches on it in a thrift shop from a very pretty, fine-boned man. (Very French!) Buying it made you feel like a more beautiful person, the grown-up version of your sixteen-year-old self. Someone who would know how to tie a scarf casually, like a Parisian, like an *adult*. The scarf cost way more than you thought because you did the conversion wrong and were too embarrassed to admit it. It was all you bought in Paris because it's all you *could* buy, you ran out of money right then and there. Sitting here on the plane, you wind the scarf around your thumb and tighten it until your thumb turns white, and then purple, strangled by peaches. It's so like you to go to Paris and buy a thing that reminds you of home, even if it's something you don't even *like*.

Josh Harris makes a snoring sound and smacks his perfect lips. You stare at him, willing him to like you back. Why can't it be that simple? You want to explain to him about the peach scarf, about yourself, about how you're more complicated and more interesting than he even could imagine.

*Moony*, you think, in Kath's voice. You flip the page and make a new drawing. The same field, surrounded by wildflowers and mountains. You add a moon, full and glowing in the top corner, and begin shading in the sky with blackness. A shooting star. Then another. And another. You draw a plaid blanket laid out on the ground, two bottles of beer, a cooler.

You close your eyes and make a wish.

You wish that *something* would happen before you land, something that would make this trip worthwhile, after all.

A story you can tell, later, one that ends with, "And that's how me and Josh Harris got together."

Ideally, that is.

In the corner of the field, you draw Josh Harris, jogging toward the picnic. Sneaking a look at Josh Harris, you see his eyes are still closed, but you angle the page away, in case he wakes up. He can't know what you're thinking: him and you, a field and a starry night.

You blush furiously, the heat of it almost making you sweat. But you keep drawing. You draw yourself on the blanket, watching him. You might be able to make the story real if you want it badly enough. That's how it works, right?

That's what Kath says and Kath is one of those girls who know what they are doing, who don't stop and ask every ten seconds, *Is this okay? Am I okay? Am I doing it right?*

Not like *you.*

You press harder. The pen makes a divot in the page.

# 2.

ON YOUR THIRD night in the hotel, you drank four cups of terrible red wine. It was four more cups of wine than you'd ever had before.

That was a mistake.

The wine stained your tongue and teeth purple, so that the next morning when you looked in the mirror, you thought something apocalyptic had happened to you in the night. You tried to Google "teeth purple am I dying" but the Wi-Fi was down, so you brushed until your gums bled, by which point you were pretty convinced you really *were* sick, spitting purple and blood into the rusted drain in the sink. Your head hurt and the room spun. Maybe it was a brain tumor.

Probably.

When you said that out loud, Kath laughed sleepily and said, "Duh, it's the wine! That always happens. It stains your teeth. Plus, you have a hangover? You're so naïve."

"Oh," you said. You pressed a cold cloth to your head, which made you feel less dizzy, if only for a few minutes. Kath's parents let her drink wine at the dinner table. Everything about her family was so grown up, so sophisticated. Somehow, you never connected wine with hangovers, just with Kath's family—three older brothers who were goofy and fun and who worshiped Kath, parents who did romantic things like waltzing around the living room—clinking glasses and smiling wide, all white teeth and high cheekbones, looking like a commercial for "How To Live Your Best Life" or tooth whiteners.

You had drunk the wine in the hallway of your hotel, which looked like every hotel you've ever stayed in on band trips, except that everything was super tiny. You leaned against one wall of the hallway and rested your feet partway up the wall on the other side and tried to ignore Charlie Martin, who kept trying to touch your hair. He was drunk.

"It looks sooooo soft," he cooed. "Like . . . uh . . . like baby hair. Or *feathers*! Feathers." He shook his head and sighed. "Bay-beeeee birdy feathers."

You were sitting close enough that his sweaty arm dampened your shirt but there was no way you could move because the wine had transformed your legs into cooked spaghetti.

"My dad doesn't love me," he said, suddenly, thickly. Then he burst into tears. "I wish I was better at sports," he slurred into your shoulder.

Charlie Martin was actually pretty athletic, for a band geek. He wasn't not-cute either. He must know that. But your brain was spongy and you couldn't make anything reassuring come out of your mouth, so you crawled away from him and into your room.

"Good night," you managed, pushing the door open with your head. "*Bonne nuit.*" You don't know where everyone had gone or when they left, the wine did something strange to time. Charlie had tipped over and begun snoring. No one else was in sight. At least he hadn't tried to kiss you. Your first kiss will be with Josh Harris. It has to be. Josh is your fate. Certainly not drunken Charlie Martin on the floor in the tiny, terrible French hotel.

In the room, there was no space between the beds and the walls or between the two beds. The bathroom was a tiny shower stall with a pedestal sink crammed beside a toilet. That's where you threw up, hitting your head on the strange pipes that stuck out over the sink. There was no room in Paris for undignified bodily functions. And you are pretty much always undignified.

Kath never is. That's why you hate/love her.

Kath is *made* for places like Paris. She'd been before because her mom is a lawyer for a cosmetics company and sometimes has to come here for work. So Kath wasn't surprised by anything Parisian: the smells, the small room, the uneven sidewalks. She moved through all of it elegantly, like a ballerina, or a fashion model on a break between shows at Fashion Week.

So even while you scrubbed at the red wine stain on your teeth, Kath lay across her bed like someone posed in a music video, still wearing her little black dress from the night before.

"Are you even awake?" you asked her. "Don't go back to sleep."

"No. Yes. I'm awake. And stop staring at me, Nerdball," she said. Her eyes stayed closed.

"I'm not staring," you said. "We're late. And I'm dying, in case you care. Why did you let me drink that stuff? Where were you, anyway? How can you possibly look *good*? I hate you."

"I don't, like, kiss and tell," she said. "Nope."

"Well, thanks for nothing," you said. "I feel like crap."

"I feel GOOD," she said. "I'm basically a woman now."

"Ugh," you said. "Hang on."

You threw up again, the acid burning your tongue, somehow stinging inside your nose. Again and again, until you were empty.

You were in Paris to play in a band festival, which turned out to be no different from every band festival in America that you'd ever been to. Parisian band students were just as awkward as all the other ones, maybe even more so. Their instruments all creaked and groaned and they, too, coughed and sneezed and waited too long to start and dropped their music. They all sucked. Or maybe it was just that everyone was good, which made it seem like no one was. The first-place band was from Sweden. They were a small group, mostly blond and thin and pale as ghosts. Their music wafted around the room like it, too, was thinner and more ethereal than everyone else's.

Your band placed third, no thanks to you. You only pretended to blow into your flute. The music that your friends played rose and fell around you and you sat there, faking it, and hating your hangover and wine and hating yourself for hating Paris and for not being self-assured and silkily confident or blond and *wafty*. Hating yourself for not measuring up to everyone else is one of your main things, right above Googling possibly deadly diseases you might have and collecting weird death stories. *Everyone needs hobbies!* That's what your mom always says, even though she probably wouldn't classify hypochondria, a fascination with the dumb ways people die, and self-loathing as the best options.

The smell of your stale metallic spit inside the flute's mouthpiece made you suddenly need to puke again, halfway through *The Prisoner's March*, a clangy piece of music that Mr. Appleby claimed to have composed. It was long and loud and in a minor key. You had to run for the exit, nearly falling into Charlie while he performed his deafening solo saxophone riff. You made it only as far as a potted plant that was stage left. Mr. Appleby caught your eye. He shook his head slowly, depressed by you and your weak stomach and lame, noiseless flute performance. "Hey," he mouthed.

*You* are why your band didn't win.

Later that day, you all took a tour of the Eiffel Tower and you fainted on the lower observation deck after you'd fallen behind the group. Something very odd happened; it was like your brain was being prickled by pins and then everything went white in slow motion. When you came around, a French security guard was nudging you with her foot. "*Ça va?*" she said. No one seemed very worried, so you got up woozily and pretended nothing had happened. Pretending awkward things didn't happen is your superpower.

It came to light later that Kath wasn't with you while you were unconscious because she was having real, actual *sex* in a bathroom with her crush object, the Right Max. That's why you lay there, dreaming, while sandaled tourists stepped over you, unconcerned. (What did they think? That you were pretending? That you were actually enjoying lying with your face pressed on the glass, Paris dizzyingly far below you?)

Kath thinks you're mad because you're *jealous*, which you aren't, not even close. The Right Max is really no better than the Other Max: His freckles crowd out his skin and he is always picking at the cuticles of his fingernails. Worse, he has dry lips that look like they'd crack and break open on impact. His breath always smells like onions or old coins.

He's definitely not in the same league as Josh Harris.

Not even close.

Later that day you saw the Right Max making out with Melody Hartwell in the lobby of the hotel. Either Kath lied to you, or Max is a worse human being than you previously thought. But you don't care, because you *fainted* at the Eiffel Tower and she wasn't there to save you. She put someone else first. She put a *boy* first. And that broke the ONE rule you two have always had: *Girls before squirrels.*

She picked a *squirrel*.

Over you!

And you were in real, genuine distress!

He wasn't even a *good* squirrel.

In that split second when you woke up, your cheek pressed against the cold smooth floor, the feet of everyone disregarding you, you were entirely alone. *Abandoned.*

You're also mad about the wine. The wine had been Kath's idea. Maybe you're allergic. Or maybe it just doesn't mix with your arthritis medication.

Anyway, Max is shorter than she is. She can do better. She *will* do better. One day. No way is she going to end up with Max Onion-Coin Breath. Not a chance. He has a future selling cars at his dad's dealership.

But Kath?

Kath has a future in everything.

# 3.

THE PLANE DIPS and you shriek, but under your breath, like a silent dream-scream, paralyzed in your mouth. What comes out sounds like a burp or a quack, a duck with indigestion.

Perfect. You roll your eyes at yourself, add one more thing to your mental list of the ways in which you are the Most Awkward Girl Alive.

That could be a great subtitle for a graphic novel about you, which maybe you should write instead of this pretty embarrassing thing about Josh Harris. *Elyse Schmidt: The Most Awkward Girl Alive*. It would be more honest.

In the book, you'd wear a cape, but you'd always be tripping over it. It could end when you fall out of a tree, trying to save a kitten. You quickly sketch a possible cover for it in your sketchbook and then slowly begin coloring in the letters with a crosshatch of black ink. There's something about the way the pen makes its soft, inky sound against the paper that calms you down, slows your pulse, makes you less aware of the fact that the only thing separating you from certain death is the metal tube that you're sitting in.

As if to emphasize this, the plane lurches again.

Josh Harris stirs but doesn't wake up. You wish he would, just so you wouldn't feel so alone, here at the back of the plane, behind all the action. You're incredibly, mind-bogglingly terrified of flying, as it turns out.

"Huh," you say, out loud. You chock it up to yet another phobia for your lengthening list. By the time you're old, your list will be long enough to stretch around the world. Of course, by then, you'll probably be agoraphobic and house-bound. You're already scared of crowds and of being touched.

You breathe in deeply. Too deeply. Are you hyperventilating? Better question: Is the plane safe? Kath could talk you down, but you aren't talking to Kath, which makes you even madder, that she could leave you alone back here, quietly freaking out.

You should have guessed that you would be afraid, seeing as how you're scared of so many things: sharks, heights, crowds, murderers, horror movies, being stuck in an elevator (unless you're with Josh Harris), accidentally eating a poisonous mushroom, ghosts, the impending apocalypse, being kidnapped and kept prisoner in some creep's basement forever, meteors hitting the Earth, what will happen if the sun burns out. Oh, and also cats. No one understands that last one, but it's the way they look at you with their slitted eyes and how they seem to be plotting your demise, or at least waiting for you to die from natural causes so they can eat you.

You stand up with your head bent awkwardly at the neck to avoid hitting it on the bulkhead. You need to see better, so you can assess if anyone else, like you, is wishing they had a paper bag to breathe into. You make yourself breathe through your nose. It's mouth breathing that causes hyperventilation, which causes fainting. You learned this from Google when you searched for "why do I get so dizzy when I'm anxious." *Life must have been very hard for people before Google*, you think.

Anyway, no one is doing anything very interesting. Mostly people are watching the same movie on their screens. Dozens of Benedict Cumberbatches tip their hats and wink. Some people are eating. A mom is comforting a baby who is crying. A lot of people are asleep. It all looks normal, or what you assume *normal* to be on a plane, so there must be no reason to worry, which does nothing to stop you from worrying.

You hate this plane.

You hate traveling.

But it's better, you suppose, to find that out now than later, after you've pinned your identity on being a free-spirited, traveling hitchhiker, sleeping in hostels and hoisting a backpack, exploring Southeast Asia and having short romances with bearded boys from Australia and Scotland. You're kind of relieved about this, actually. It's one more person you don't have to be. There are so many options. Ruling any of them out makes the whole prospect of "deciding who you're going to be" *slightly* less arduous. Besides which, no one gets murdered more frequently than free-spirited hitchhikers.

You pop your earbuds back in and crank the Hoppers. Josh Harris has been wearing a Hoppers T-shirt and you'd thought that, maybe, the Hoppers could be something you have in common, a band you could go see together. If. When.

The trouble is that they are terrible. The violin bows scratch chalkboard-squeaky against the strings, sawing back and forth until your teeth clench so hard your jaw pings. You pause the sound, but you leave the earbuds in, dialing through some options. Your dad has uploaded his favorite song, which is by Guns N' Roses: "Sweet Child O' Mine." He used to sing it to you all the time when you were a baby. You smile. Your dad is a goofball and you miss him and you can't wait to see him. When the song ends, you hit pause and listen to nothing. *Nothing* is probably exactly what you and Josh Harris have in common, after all. If only you could get sort of comfortable, maybe you could sleep. You shift but you're careful to keep your arm on your side of the armrest. You're careful not to touch him. Because, *Josh Harris*. Josh Harris! If this were a graphic novel, there would be an exclamation mark floating over your head for the entire duration of the flight. You flip the page in your sketchbook and quickly draw yourself in this very seat. Then you draw an exclamation mark over the *you* on the page. You widen your eyes. Then you draw Josh Harris, staring at you *moonily*. You draw a thought bubble over his head.

*Elyse Schmidt is adorable!* you write.

Ha. You wish.

You scribble over it quickly and thoroughly. Where is the line between a crush and full-on crazy? That's the question Kath keeps asking that you should also ask yourself.

You allow yourself to look at him properly for the first time since you sat down and then you blush. Again. You can feel the heat of it creeping up your neck, onto your cheeks, making your eyes water. You look out the window to distract yourself. There is nothing to see but white clouds thinning and thickening and thinning again, which reminds you of how you fainted at the Eiffel Tower, how everything first turned white and then the whiteness wouldn't let you go. Even thinking about the Eiffel Tower makes you lightheaded and pissed off. Now you'll be like one of Pavlov's dogs, fainting every time you see it on TV or in a movie. Great. You put your sketchpad into the seat pocket in front of you and stare at it, your favorite pen clipped to the front. Then you take it out again. You can't stop yourself.

The graphic novel you are slowly, *almost* accidentally, creating is called *ME AND JOSH HARRIS: A LOVE STORY*, a title that was sort of meant to be a joke but also not exactly funny. How can something you want so bad be a punch line?

"That's bananas," Kath said, when you showed her. "You should at least change his name."

"I can't. Then it wouldn't be real. Anyway, it feels more proactive than mooning. It's like that book *The Secret*. I can secret it into being true. Maybe. Theoretically. Anyway, isn't it better to turn it into, like, creative output? It's not like I'm going to get it published or something. It's not like he'll ever *see* it."

"Imagine if you do sell it!" She started laughing. "And his dad orders it for the bookstore and then says, 'Son, this book has your name on it!' Then they open up the first page and realize that it *is* him, and *you*, and—" She had to stop talking because she was laughing too hard to continue. Then she made that "you're nuts" sign with her finger, twirling it at her temple, crossing her eyes.

"Stop!" But you were laughing, too.

It was funny. It *is* funny.

But it is also maybe *true love*.

You flip to a clean page and start drawing a random scene. It's like drawing your daydreams. It doesn't mean anything, it just comes to you, a fleshed-out scene, and you feel compelled to put it on paper. This one is you and Josh Harris at some kind of a dance. You're wearing a strapless dress. He's wearing a tux but the tie is half hanging off. If Kath saw it, she'd get the giggles again. "You have no idea what having a boyfriend is really like!" she'd say. "I love eighties movies, but real relationships are not like Molly Ringwald and Andrew McCarthy staring longingly into each other's eyes! Fully half of any relationship is feeling annoyed that the other person hasn't texted you or if they gave you a cold sore or something. Did you know cold sores are really herpes?"

Kath is an expert because for three months—August, September, and October—she was "in a relationship" with

Charlie "your hair is like baby feathers" Martin. Poor Charlie. She didn't *sleep* with him, though. She barely even let him touch her. If she did have *sex* with the Right Max, it's big news. BIG NEWS, all caps. *You* don't feel old enough to have sex. You aren't ready. How can she be ready when you're not?

Anyway, this is just *fiction* that you're drawing. It's fantasy, not real life. It doesn't have to include the boring parts or the irritation, which you know exists. You live with your parents, for goodness' sake. They fight constantly. They can turn a perfectly normal question like, "Is there any orange juice in the fridge?" into a reason to draw up divorce papers.

But you don't want to *marry* Josh Harris. You want to fall in love with him. That's different.

You go back to your drawing and add confetti falling from the ceiling. You draw people watching you dance, clapping like you're winning some kind of dance contest in an old-fashioned movie, where you'll get a trophy and your photo in the local paper. You give yourself Molly Ringwald's hair.

Sometimes you think you were born in the wrong generation. Everything about the now is too techy, too modern, too fast, too soon. You barely even like texting. If you had a choice, you'd always "forget" your phone. It just seems like so much trouble to stop what you're doing, to type things out painstakingly with your thumb, which is usually aching. Maybe the people who like it just don't have Junky Idiotic Arthritis.

You draw a big banner on the page: THE GREAT 1980s DANCE-OFF. You add some ruffles to your dress to make it look more '80s. You make your hair bigger. You give Josh

Harris wild, huge hair, but it's obviously a wig, slipping sideways on his skull. Come to think of it, there aren't a lot of black people in those '80s movies.

You'll have to tell Kath when she's talking to you again. She must have noticed. How many black people were there in *Say Anything? Sixteen Candles? Pretty in Pink?*

Zero.

"That *sucks*," you mutter, and add a bunch more people of all different races into your drawing, but you don't add Kath. "You aren't invited," you tell the back of her head. "You can go hump Max in the bathroom."

You keep your body angled to hide the pad from Josh Harris. If he were to wake up, he would see what you are drawing and you would die. Instantly. People die in weird ways all the time. They say that no one has ever died of embarrassment but you know differently. A maid in the 1800s was caught stealing in front of a group of people and she collapsed right there, dead. The cause of death was officially recorded as "embarrassment," although maybe it was less true embarrassment and more adrenalin and probably something like Long QT syndrome, which you know a lot about because you're pretty sure you have it, and one day in gym class, you'll keel over dead yourself.

Anyway, if Josh Harris knew how obsessed you were with him, you'd get a pretty big jolt of adrenaline, too, and then . . . flatline.

You close the sketchbook. Sitting here for eleven more hours seems impossible and also like heaven, because of *him*.

The window has a tiny hole in the outer layer of it. You put your nose closer to it, to try to breathe fresh air. The air outside must be as sharp as mountain air, or what you imagine mountain air would be like, which is just *better*: cleaner, colder, fresher. You press your finger against the little hole. The window feels ice cold. The hole is definitely there on purpose, but why? It seems dangerous to have that there, a pinhole opening between you and the open sky. You picture it spidering open, like a windshield crack, then collapsing, the vacuum it created pulling you out into nothingness.

You want to say something about the hole to Josh Harris.

He's still sleeping. You want to touch him so bad. Before you can stop it, your hand casually reaches out on its own accord and rests on Josh Harris's leg, which jumps like the frog that you had to pith in biology class two weeks ago. You quickly pull your hand back and frown at it.

You should probably pith your hand. Are hands pithable?

You say the word *pith* out loud, which is strangely satisfying. *Pith, pith, pith.* It's a much gentler word than *murder.* You think about karma and about how that frog died, his tiny chest heaving, looking for air that wasn't there. You think about Josh Harris, who is so stupidly gorgeous, even when he's sleeping. Maybe especially when he's sleeping.

Thinking about Josh Harris is the background soundtrack of your life, an entire album called *Thinking about Josh Harris.*

The one good thing about Paris is that you have a whole new set of memories of Josh Harris to add to your growing collection. Moments when you caught his eye; casual things he said to you. Like, "Schmidt, did you see Fitzy throwing up those poor, small snails? They died for no reason. Tragic, right?" Then the time he caught your eye across the restaurant where you were picking at a plate of dry chicken (wasn't French food supposed to be sooooo good?) and held it for a good ten seconds too long, then grinned and you knew exactly what he meant. The highlight: Sharing an elevator with him (and five other people) and during the ride down to the lobby, he rested his hand on your head in a way that made you never want to move again. That had to mean something. What did it mean? Does Josh Harris like you? Maybe a little? Or is it just that you're so short and he's so tall that it's where his hand naturally landed?

You wish you could analyze the head pat with Kath, but not talking to her is making that impossible, which makes you even more mad at her. Thinking about it, the head pat could even be offensive. You pat dogs. You pat goats. You don't pat *people*. That can't ever be good.

*Talk to me!* you want to yell at Kath. *Turn around and apologize so we can get back to normal! There was a head pat! Did you really have sex? What is happening to* us? *Girls before squirrels! Duh!*

You look at Josh Harris again, the curve of his cheek, the stubble where he's shaved his head and his hair is trying to grow back. He smells like boy-deodorant and clean sheets and toast. You pull the smell into you and hold your breath and then feel too creepy for words, so you exhale. You could just put your head on his shoulder and fall asleep. You want to do that so bad.

Josh, like you, plays the flute. He plays basketball *and* he plays the flute. He is six foot something tall and has the most gorgeous lips you've ever seen and is the opposite of you in every way, except for that one thing: flute playing. He wears his beauty so casually, it's like he's forgotten he has it. Sort of like Kath, come to think of it. They'd look good together. They'd look *amazing.* You are suddenly even more furious with her, which you know is unfair, but you can't help it. It's like your anger is a piece of yarn being pulled from a sweater that keeps unraveling more and more and more. Now everything is a mess and you want to bop her on the back of her dancing head for being gorgeous and self-assured and tall and confident, all things you are not. You stick out your tongue instead.

Josh Harris is wearing an old T-shirt and jeans that he makes look like stuff everyone else would pay any amount of money for, if only it were for sale. Even the flute becomes something brighter than a flute when he blows into it. It's not just you who thinks so, Mr. Appleby does, too. Josh is better than you by far, even though you—being very small—*look* like someone who would play the flute, like some kind of elf in a fairy tale. And you practice *constantly.* He doesn't. He just plays. Things want to be played by Josh Harris.

"*You are too much,*" Kath says, in your head. You know her so well after all these years of being BFFs that you don't even need her to actually say the things you know she would say. It's like you've got a mini-Kath who has taken up residence in your head. "*If I roll my eyes much harder I'm going to pull my optical nerves right out of my brain and have to go through life with a glass eye and a lot of resentment."*

Josh Harris's eyelashes are about a half inch long. You've never noticed them before. You sit on your hands so they don't reach out and touch them. "Schmidt," you say to yourself. "Keep it together."

Josh Harris has always been famous in your school for terrible reasons. You hadn't known him when it happened, but you'd heard about it. Everyone had. A home invasion. His mom, murdered. He did a speech last fall at school about it. Hearing it from his own mouth turned you inside out. He had been playing, he said. A game he played by himself while his parents were in the front room, watching their favorite show on TV. He had heard the glass breaking and instead of running to see what happened, he had hidden in the corner of his playroom behind a huge houseplant. "The leaves were so big, just one could nearly cover me," he said. "It made me feel invisible. I felt like a superhero, except I could do nothing to save my mom." Josh Harris has a very meticulous way of speaking that makes you think of bedsheets, cornered perfectly. Before his dad bought the bookstore, he had been a stage actor. You imagine Josh's dad teaching him to project his voice. You picture them reading out loud from *Macbeth* in front of a fireplace, his tweed-jacketed dad *e-nun-see-ate-ing* clearly and little Josh Harris, mimicking that. Basically, you want to climb into his voice and live there.

Josh Harris said that when the police came, he still didn't move. He waited for his dad's voice, calling his name over and over again from the stretcher just before he was lifted into the back of the ambulance. His mother was already dead. He said that he went over to where she was lying under a sheet and he lifted it and kissed her goodbye. He was only six! No one is that calm when they are six. No one. But you could believe that Josh Harris was. He's *different*. That's all there is to it. He is a person who would be good in a crisis, able to handle anything, able to survive.

He would always remember to kiss you goodbye.

After he finished speaking, the entire class was so quiet, you could hear breathing. No one spoke, to avoid sobbing out loud, even the teacher. Everyone, even the Right Max, who almost always had something smart-assy to say, sat in complete silence for at least two minutes, maybe more (it felt like forever), until the bell went and they could leave. Josh Harris looked perfectly fine. He was the only one. Everyone else looked stricken. He didn't seem to notice. "Yo Fitzy," he'd said. "Let's go shoot some hoops."

You've never forgotten that day.

That was the day when you fell in love.

And you haven't stopped loving him ever since, not for a minute.

That's how you know it's real.

You are Elyse Schmidt who loves Josh Harris, period. It's who you are.

# 4.

Up until October, Josh Harris was with Danika Prefontaine, who is repulsively, sickeningly blond and bubbly and pretty, like someone from a show on the Disney Channel who can sing and dance and generally look gorgeous in all things, at all times. She plays the oboe. She's also a cheerleader and has smoothly perfect, glowing skin that must be makeup or a miracle or both. You have no idea what she puts on it to get it like that, but whatever it is, you want it. Probably, it's nothing. She is just a person who *sparkles*. Someone said she got pregnant and had an abortion, but people say that about everyone who dates for more than a few weeks. It is obviously never true (that you know of), or at least, rarely. You need for it to not be true about Danika because you need for their connection to not have mattered. Something like that would have made it bigger than it was.

Besides, it's over. You know that for sure.

Josh Harris is free.

When Josh Harris wakes up, maybe you'll talk to him. When he wakes up, maybe he'll grin at you and say, "Oh hey, Schmidt."

When he wakes up, maybe he'll notice you, really *see* you.

Maybe you will even ask him to stop calling you Schmidt. No one sounds pretty when they are being called Schmidt. It sounds too phlegmy. You say your first name out loud. "Elyse." Elyse is a pretty name. It's fine. It's not the best name in the world, but it's definitely not the worst. You've never been an "Ellie" or a "Lisa" or anything, always Elyse.

"Elyse Schmidt," you say, your voice swallowed up by the roar of the engine and all the plane and people sounds. You make the Schmidt sound like you are choking on a sharp bone. You try it again, like a sneeze. Josh Harris is a heavy sleeper.

Kath kneels up and peers over the back of her seat to look at you and says, "Stop talking to yourself, Schmidt."

She spits on the *Schmidt*, speckling your pretty-nerd glasses. The glasses may have been a mistake. "Those glasses are trying too hard," Kath had said, when she saw them for the first time. "Those glasses say, 'I am quirky! Love me!' Too desperate. Also, they are so big, they make you look even smaller, like a shrunken head, and I mean that in the nicest way. You are dwarfed by your eyewear."

*Sleepy, Grumpy, Dopey, Nope-y,* you'd thought. "Don't say 'dwarfed.' It makes you sound racist or something."

"I'm black," she'd said.

"Well, you can still be dwarfist."

"But some of my best friends are dwarfs!" She laughed. "See what I did there? Don't look like that! I'm kidding. God. Lighten up."

But the thing is that you *are* pretty short. Four foot eleven and a half. Five feet in sneakers. Just. If you stand up extra-straight.

You kept the glasses, stubbornly, even though she was probably right. Sometimes you resented when she told you that you were doing it wrong. Like when she laughed at the way you bought a hundred of the same temporary tattoo— the one that said BE BRAVE—and reapplied it every day for a year. When she rolled her eyes at the T-shirts you wore, advertising your favorite YouTube artists' channels. One day, you might even work up the nerve to have your own, but you can't figure out the banter part of it, just the drawing.

Anyway, you are only wearing the glasses right now because your contacts got so dry on the way over that by the time you landed, your eyes were as red as ink and all of Paris was a blur of lights against darkness. Part of having Junky Idiotic Arthritis is that your eyes are very prone to uveitis, an inflammation that makes it feel like your eyelids are made of sandpaper, scraping, scraping, scraping. You aren't really sure what one has to do with the other, but inflammation is inflammation and it sucks wherever it is.

"I hate you," you remind Kath now. You take off your glasses and wipe them on your shirt. "I'm not talking to you."

"Well, *pith* you, Elyse Schmidt," she says, loudly. "Did you know that talking to yourself is one of the earliest signs of dementia? You should Google it. Pretty soon, you probably won't remember who I am. But don't worry, I'll still feed you mushed bananas and tell someone when you need your diaper changed. Because even though I'm mad at you, I'm—"

"Shhh," you say, gesturing at Josh Harris.

Josh Harris is drooling. Kath makes a kissing face at him and licks her lips.

Then she stage-whispers, "KISS HIM, YOU FOOL." There's something about being on a plane that makes you feel like you aren't quite yourself. Like you could *almost* bring yourself to do it, but not quite. "You know," Kath says, "I was thinking—"

Then, SUDDENLY, with Kath dangling awkwardly over the back of her seat, mid-sentence, the plane TILTS.

All caps, like that.

And Kath disappears.

The interruption is so abrupt that you lose your place in yourself, as though you're a book that you've just dropped on the floor, halfway through a sentence. A book *has* dropped on the floor, in fact. It must be Josh Harris's book. You stare at it. Half the cover is missing. *Wa a Pea,* it says. Then it, too, disappears, sliding away down the row of seats.

*Wait*, you want to say. *Hang on.*

Nothing quite makes sense.

The FASTEN SEAT BELT sign flashes on. Yellow plastic masks drop down from the ceiling with a noise that makes you instantly imagine the phrase "a smattering of applause."

All the bodies take a second to catch up to what has happened. There is a lot of thumping. A drink cart has smashed into Mr. Appleby. The flight attendant has vanished, as if into thin air.

"HEY," Mr. Appleby shouts.

There is a silence as the plane seems to hang in midair, entirely motionless, for whole seconds. People are frantically clipping masks to their faces. Kath's is just swinging. Where is Kath? The plane is distinctly on its side now.

"Kath?" you scream, but your voice disappears into the yellow plastic cup that's over your face.

It is all happening very fast.

Josh Harris's eyes are wide open.

Josh Harris is staring at you.

Josh Harris's eyes are accusatory, as if you, Elyse Schmidt, are causing the plane to tilt and do what it is doing, which is very definitely falling. You shrug by way of explanation, because it is all you can do, but he probably can't tell that you are shrugging because everyone's limbs are everywhere, like gravity has given up on the entire cabin full of people. Your arm flaps up on its own accord and you have to force it back to your side. The whole situation feels too surreal to be real. You might be crying. There is definitely no leaf to hide behind right now.

What will Josh Harris do? You don't want him to die. You haven't loved him enough yet.

The plane chooses that moment to roll. For some reason, your hair is in your mouth, which means the mask has fallen off. You pull the hair out. The mask is on the ceiling, you can't reach it, but you're still breathing. Why is it windy in here? You squint at the hole in the window, in case it has splintered open. It looks intact. Josh Harris is squeezing the life out of your arm. Well, Josh Harris is welcome to break your arm if it makes him feel better, because it doesn't matter, because you are going to die. He reaches up and shoves the mask hard onto your face, which doesn't matter either.

You're going to *die*. Things are already whitening. You'll be relieved to faint because then you will be spared the details. That sounds okay right now, given the options.

If you die, your parents will be *really* upset. That's an understatement. They'll be *devastated*. They will never get over this, you know that as clearly as you know anything. You are their whole life. Well, you and the peaches.

Sometimes the peaches trump you.

Stupid peaches.

But, anyway, without you, they will for sure get divorced and spend the rest of time hating each other. You are the glue that holds them together.

"Sorry," you say out loud. "Just try harder. Share your interests or something. Be nicer to each other."

This split second is being held and stretched like taffy and on that long stretched string of time standing still, you can think whatever you want.

*I don't even* like *peaches*, is what you think.

*I'm going to die*, is what you think, *without ever going to Wyoming.*

*I love you*, is what you think.

*I'm sorry*, is what you think.

You are less scared than you would have thought.

"I love you," you say directly and loudly to Josh Harris, but he doesn't hear you. That's probably for the best. He's saying something you can't make out. It might be a prayer.

He pulls his mask off and says loudly, "I do not fear death," and then he snaps it back on. "I do not fear death," he keeps shouting, behind the mask. He looks scared. He takes his mask off again.

You shake your head. "Don't do that!" For some reason, his mouth is open. You can see his teeth, all the way to the back. There are small bumps on his tongue that look like velvet. *That's a weird thing to think about*, you think. And then time snaps like an elastic band and the plane is falling or spinning or both and, of course, you are going to die and now you are scared, too.

*I don't want to die*, you think, but the thought feels pointless.

*I do fear death*, you think. (Also, pointless.)

*Mom.* (Pointless.)

The falling keeps happening. You never got a pony. You never went to Wyoming. You never fell in love. You never decided who you were going to be. You never finished your graphic novel. You didn't get to live long enough to warrant an autobiography. You never thought of a good name for the YouTube channel that you never started.

There is something like puking and fainting and screaming all happening to you at the same time. The screaming is all around you, like a kind of tornado of sound, and you find yourself willing the inevitable crash to just *happen* so the noise will stop in addition to the strange pulling feeling that stretches down your spine and up into your brain. You don't want to die but you don't want to hear or feel *this* anymore either. That's a conundrum. *Conundrum* is a word that makes you think of umbrellas.

*Now is not the time to think of umbrellas*, you think. Then you can't think of anything else: Red, yellow, green, spotted, striped, clear umbrellas cloud your vision. An umbrella with yellow duckies. An umbrella covered in a map of the world.

There is too much air everywhere, whipping around you. You are shivering now, hard, but you're also hot, sweating. Death is coming like a rapid-fire fever.

You offer up a quick prayer, some kind of barter with God, knowing even while you do it that it's futile. *I'll do anything? Please?* you think, then you say out loud, "Please save Josh Harris. And me. Amen." But you understand randomness and how this particular bit of randomness means you're going to die. Randomness is something you can believe in. Death is on its way to you.

Slowly.

Faster.

At a confusing speed.

You are so dizzy.

You will die in a minute. Less.

At sixteen.

Without ever having kissed Josh Harris.

You never thought you'd be a girl whose last thought was about kissing. Or umbrellas. You feel dumb about ever having worried about getting cancer or having Long QT syndrome or Epstein-Barr virus or possibly dying when a spotted eagle ray breached out of the water and hit you in the head while on a boat in Florida, which actually happened to a woman in 2008. You are a little disappointed to be dying in such a normal way. "Plane crash" in no way can measure up to the guy who died when a snake's decapitated head bit him while he was preparing a meal (of snake) somewhere in China.

"I am going to die in a plane crash," you say or think or both, who knows anymore.

You can suddenly, clearly see the cover of *People* magazine, with the class pictures of you and all these other soon-to-be-dead band geeks.

You lean sideways, which is hard because of the way the plane is shaking, like it's about to tear apart from the inside out. Your masks are gone, you don't know where they went or when. You put your lips on Josh's, which is nearly impossible to do, as there is the g-force and the fact that he is shaking almost as hard as the plane itself. His mouth tastes stale, but still, in that split second, you're glad to have done it.

"Schmidt," he says. You hear that so clearly, it's like you are alone, the two of you, somewhere else, and not on a crowded, crashing plane.

"It's *Elyse*," you think you say.

Your head seems to be facing your own chest and your voice isn't working. You're wearing your favorite orange T-shirt. You're going to die in this T-shirt that you love that reminds you of Orange Rabbit, the stuffed toy that you slept with every night for the first ten years of your life, the one that still sits on the shelf by your bed. You wish so hard you were on your bed, holding Orange Rabbit. You want your mom. You look briefly at the freckled skin on your arm between Josh's beautiful fingers and you think, "Well, good-bye." Your BE BRAVE tattoo is mostly washed off, but you can see crumbs of ink, clinging on. You're almost glad that you're dying with Josh's hand on you, like that. This is the best of your last moments, falling in a plane, but not alone. With Josh Harris!

You are aware of not thinking big enough or serious enough thoughts and also that you've had an awfully long time to think them, so maybe none of this is happening or maybe it's all a dream. You feel fleetingly good about the fact that it's a dream. It's not a great dream, but at least it will end, all your thoughts coming as hard and fast as plate glass that's been shattered by a bullet.

Then the mountain rises up and crashes into the plane with such unimaginable force that it's impossible that anything is happening except that you are being physically torn apart, every molecule of you tearing away from every other molecule of you, raggedly. You wish you couldn't feel it. You are jarred entirely out of yourself, and then you are still strapped into your chair, but also you are on the ceiling of the plane, deciding. There is a lot of blood everywhere, and an eerie silence.

You are aware of deciding.

Live or die.

Which one?

*Choose.*

# 5.

A LOT OF things hurt. The word *hurt* is not even close to being enough. What you're feeling isn't pain; it's more than that. It is nothing. It is everything. It is a scream, deep inside you, echoing against the walls of every cell of you, burning.

Death is right there, beckoning, cool and bright and quiet, like soft sheets on a perfectly made bed.

Your bed. You can practically see it, glowing there.

Inviting you to rest.

Except it's not your bed in your room at home, it's somewhere else. A room imagined at another time. A perfect room.

*Safe*, you think.

Then there is a smell of something burning. It smells like hair.

You retch and retch and then instantly you are back in your body and unbuckling your seat belt and something is sticky all over your face that must be blood. You can only see through one eye and even that view looks wrong, like you're looking through a kaleidoscope, a blurry one, but no point worrying about that now.

There is only this moment.

There is only *getting out.*

You know you must get out, but that's made easier by the fact that the part of the plane where you are sitting seems to be separated from the rest of the plane. In front of you, there is nothing. There is open space. *This may or may not be a dream*, you think. But you have to think it isn't. It can't be. Dreams don't hurt.

You unbuckle and you fall forward, as though you are diving off a diving board and into a pool, only there is no water in the pool and it's awfully far away, but you can't think about that, you are already falling. How is that happening? The air rushes by you and chides you for making this stupid choice.

Your leg makes a distinctive snapping sound that you feel as much as hear when you hit the ground, and you begin to roll. The ground is a slope. There is an imperative to get down the slope. You don't know why you know this, but you do. You roll and roll. It hurts so much it almost doesn't hurt, or rather, you have become pain, so adding more makes no difference. You have nothing left to lose. There is literally nothing but you, the ground, the excruciating agony of everything, and the fact that you know you have to get away from the plane, down and away.

Luckily, the slope is steep. You used to roll like this down the hill behind your house. On the green grass, freshly mowed, blue sky, green grass, blue sky, green grass, laughing. You think about root beer popsicles and the way the sun made rainbows in the sprinklers and your heart breaks into a million pieces. You think of how bees sometimes landed on your sticky fingers, their feet taking small, ticklish steps.

You aren't laughing now.

You have to roll.

Faster, faster.

Hurry, hurry.

Escape, escape, escape.

The ground has some snow and patches of ice and some rocks and lots of pebbles and some tiny branches of shrubbery that scratch you. The scratching reminds you that you're alive.

The rolling goes on and on. There is so much pain. There is the smell of jet fuel that is so strong it is closing your throat. You are going too slowly, it is taking forever to make your body move. You will still die whether or not you keep fighting. You can't breathe. So why are you still rolling? You can't give up, that's the thing. Your only remaining purpose is in the rolling. It's hard work. Your leg screams into a great stretching pain that is all over you, spandex-tight, refusing to let go. The grass passes by your face in ragged clumps.

Grass/sky/gravel/grass/sky/life/death/life/death/now/then/now/then.

There is a sudden heat.

A huge heat. It is so big, you feel engulfed. It is searing. *Searing* is a word you understand better now than ever before.

The impossible heat is also a sound, out of tune and too loud, and then the broken pieces of the plane become a sun and you are free-falling again, this time down a ravine, cool dirt walls rubbing smoothly at your skin. Above you, a ball of fire whooshes by, enormous and red.

*What the actual* fuck *was that?* you think.

In real life, you never ever swear. It's one of your *things* that makes Kath roll her eyes. So you must be dead. But if you were dead, nothing would hurt. If this were a dream, it would be painless and blurry, disconnected, with no sharp edges and twangs. But it can't possibly be real. It's too hard to logic it out. Not death, not a dream, not real, then what?

*Stop thinking*, you instruct yourself. *Just breathe.*

The heat and the smell and the smoke are suffocating you and the pain is in so many places you can't tell where it is coming from and the sky is gone and the ground is gone and you are gone. Are you gone?

No.

You don't die.

You aren't dead.

You are the ground and the sky and the burning plane, your cells spread everywhere at once and yet still contained within your skin. It's impossible but it's possible.

You are everything.

You are nothing.

You are stuck in yourself with all this pain, the blue sky black smoke red fire all melted into one enormously impossible agony of ugly colors and knife blades.

But.

*But . . .*

Here is a miracle:

*Josh Harris isn't dead either.*

You know this, because he is underneath you. You have landed on Josh Harris. Josh Harris is definitely no longer conscious, but he is *alive.* You can feel him breathing. You know he is not dead. You rise up and down gently in a way that makes you think of floating on the surface of a lake on an air mattress in another life, *before.*

Now you are the thing that is between Josh Harris and death.

You are the leaf.

"I am the leaf," you try to tell him, but something is in your mouth: blood and shattered teeth. You retch.

The sky is nothing but black smoke now. The blue is gone. Pain is everywhere. Somehow you are still breathing even though every breath is scented with smoke and poison. But the air directly around you is below all that. It is wet and smells like clay. You lie still both because you can't move and because *you are the leaf*, and that is a job you take seriously. The burning feeling is unbearable but the interior of you is cool and soft and the sky is bluing again already, forcing the black gray white to dissipate into its greater blueness. Your brain isn't allowing anything to make sense and is doing something strange and sticky to the word *blue.*

Poor Josh Harris.

You are on your side. Only one eye will open. You look through your one eye and you can see that your leg is bent in a way that isn't possible. Still a dream then. No, not a dream. Too painful. Everything is very blurry and thick, even the air you are trying to breath.

You slip in and out of sleep, as though it is a door that you are trying to force open, an elevator door. You want to get in! The door keeps sliding shut, rejecting you. *Blue*, you think. If you can get a dream to start and catch, then you can sleep and then wake up and this can be over. Josh Harris makes strange sounds, ducks in his throat, velvet on his lips.

*Shhhh, Josh Harris*, you say, inside your head, because your mouth isn't working. You sleep and wake up. Wake up and sleep. It's not sleep. It is something heavier than that, with more static, a roaring in your ears that won't stop, like the echo of what just happened. You open your eyes and the roar lessens.

You watch the smoke gradually filter entirely away, leaving the sky's blue supremacy to reign again, as though a plane hasn't just torn through it and ripped it into pieces. It's strange how there is no tear showing, how it closed itself back up again seamlessly. You don't know how much time has passed. You can hear someone moaning, which means someone else is alive, or maybe the moaning is coming from you. Who could possibly have survived?

(Not Mr. Appleby. Not either Max. Not Melody. Not Danika Prefontaine. Not Fitzy. Not Charlie Martin. Not Kath. Not the angry British girl. Definitely not the flight attendant.)

You think about the people who did not live—you know that definitely people died—although you don't know yet how long that list of names will be. You imagine them all now holding hands, slipping smoothly between the blue molecules of the sky ceiling, vanishing into an ether of light. You have never been so aware of how the light is there, waiting for all of you. You've never understood so clearly how easily you could become part of the flow of that eternal river of endless light. But Josh Harris isn't going and so neither are you. In that way, he is saving you, too.

You lie there for a long time, watching the sky give up its hold on *blue* and fade to gray while serenely accepting their souls, then turning darker from the weight of all of them. It gets quieter and quieter. There's a wind. It's intensely cold.

The absolute silence pours over you like water in an ice-cold creek and you slip into it, crisp and perfect against your burning skin. You let it take you, just for now. You don't know what else to do. What *is* there to do? Your mouth tastes like blood and oil and your dream is shattered around the edges like the flickering lights of a migraine and you need a drink of water and you can't take a deep breath without your lungs crumpling like tinfoil.

You fall asleep thinking about the sky and why you've never properly noticed it before, the stars punching holes in the blackness, showing the people who just arrived in the light a glimpse of the dark, silent world they have left behind.

part two

# 6.

THIS IS WHAT dreams look like when they come true:

You and Josh Harris are lying on a blanket on a football field in Wyoming. The blanket is plaid and smooth and smells like fabric softener. The air is heavy with the scent of wildflowers and summer and tree pollen and, faintly, lawn mower gas and sawdust.

Above you, the sky is clear and warm and star-freckled. There's supposed to be a meteor shower tonight, which you remember, as if waking from a dream, is *why* you are here with Josh Harris and a backpack filled with snacks and a tiny cooler full of melting ice and six green glass bottles of beer, which you don't really like but will drink anyway because tonight, one of the last summer nights before school starts up, the night of *the biggest meteor shower in history*, is going to be the most important night of your life, so far.

The *best* night of your life, so far.

The most romantic night of your life, so far.

"I used to be afraid of meteors," you say. Your voice comes out froggy. You clear your throat.

"Who's afraid of meteors?" He turns to look at you and his face makes you feel light-headed. It's so close to you. So close. And you could kiss him right now if you wanted to, because Josh Harris is your boyfriend.

Instead of kissing him, you lean up on your elbow. "Not the meteors, but the possibility that they could, like, slam into the Earth and erase all of mankind."

"Oh, *that*."

"Yeah, that. No one wants to be . . . made extinct. There's probably a word for that." You're sitting up now, crisscross applesauce, like in kindergarten on the alphabet carpet. You can practically smell the carpet fibers, artificial and somehow chemical.

"Extinguished?"

"Extinguished," you repeat. "Yes. That's a terrible word." You close your eyes. You used to Google things like "anticipated trajectory of asteroid Apophis." (Apophis has a 2.7 percent chance of crashing into the Earth in 2029, when you will only be 29 and won't really have finished being who you are going to be yet.)

"But you're not scared of them anymore, right?"

"I guess I'm not scared of anything anymore," you tell him, uncrossing your legs.

52

You don't have to tell him why. After all, if you live to be twenty-nine, you'll have had thirteen bonus years past the time when you should have died, but didn't.

He pulls you down next to him and you land awkwardly on your elbow, which seems to have nowhere to go. You tuck it under your side. "I get it," he says.

"I know."

"That's because you *get* me."

"We *get* each other."

He smiles and his smile and the way his two top teeth overlap the tiniest bit is so familiar to you, you suddenly don't know where he begins and you end. "Cue the romantic music!" he says and he starts humming something sweet.

It's like that.

You didn't really know Josh Harris *Before*.

You had an *idea* of who he was, who you wanted him to be, but you had no way of being sure who he really was beyond being gorgeous and good at all things. You assumed he was nice, but did you really know? He just seemed like a person who would help elderly people with their groceries at the store, like someone who would risk his own life to save a dog from a river or something. You assumed he liked animals. You assumed he was a good kisser.

And, well, you weren't *totally* wrong. So maybe he hasn't changed as much as you did, after all. But as it turns out, he doesn't like animals. He's afraid of them, he's told you. Dogs, cats, all of them, but especially horses, which is too bad for you. "Animals are unpredictable," he says. "I like to know what's going to happen next."

You like that he is afraid of something. (Even though you wish it wasn't horses.) It makes him seem more human. It makes him seem more like you. Besides, even if he were afraid, he'd still pull a dog out of the rapids, you're sure of it.

Now, *After*, you are a completely different person and probably he is, too, but the ways that you've both changed fit perfectly together. Somehow.

Magically.

You turn your head away from him slightly, which makes him disappear. The eye on the side of your face closest to him is gone.

Lost forever. You sometimes imagine it on the side of the mountain, still staring up at that same sky. Sometimes you feel like you can almost see what it sees.

Of course, that's not how it was. It was damaged and removed by surgeons, cleanly, in an operating room some-time during the aftermath, a surging tide of time that comes back to you only in tiny fits and starts.

Being able to see out of only one eye gives you a strange perspective. You're getting used to it, but still, sometimes you fall up stairs and bash into furniture when you misjudge the angles.

But even losing an eye was not the biggest change. The bigger change is inside you.

You can't explain it. You are still a hypochondriac and you are still self-loathing, but you are also so much braver and sharper, as though the crash carved off your dull edges, leaving you as glistening and dangerous as a razor. Additionally, you are shockingly pale and *wafty*, like a Swedish piccolo player. All of your curves and lumps dissolved away while you were sleeping or in a coma or having surgery to pin the bones in your body back together.

After the crash, your hair fell out and then grew in silvery-white, as thin and transparent as you felt, yet as strong as a cobweb. There is a name for the condition, which is alopecia areata. You know that you are not your hair, and yet because your hair is one of the first things that people notice about you, in a way, you are. You are the girl with the silver hair. You are the girl who was dead and is now alive.

You are the one who lived.

You are still short, obviously.

You still have Junky Idiotic Arthritis and different-but-the-same trying-too-hard glasses and parents who fight more than they dance (they never dance) and you still feel like you are better at drawing your life than living it.

So actually, you are the same.

But Josh Harris is your boyfriend.

You are Josh Harris's girlfriend.

So you aren't the same at all. You used to be someone who *yearned*. And now you're not. You're someone who already has what she always wanted.

It's taking some getting used to and it's hard to figure it out sometimes because your brain does not work quite the same as it did before. And of course getting what you always wanted came at an impossible price.

You can't think about the price.

You just can't.

# 7.

WHEN YOU FIRST got back to California, there were reporters everywhere everywhere everywhere. It was surreal, the way they kept popping up, in front of you, microphones outstretched.

You were on the *Today* show. You were on *60 Minutes*. You were on CNN. You did the *Ellen DeGeneres Show. Jimmy Kimmel.* You know these things happened because you've seen the recordings, but you don't really remember any of them in the way that you thought you would. It's slippery, the memory of it. You try to grab hold of it and it slithers away like mercury.

You've watched footage and tried to recall details—the texture of the couch you sat on or the coldness of the air-conditioning in the studio, but there is nothing there, not really. It's as if you wrote down a dream that you had, and then, rereading it, could no longer remember what it was about the dream that was so terrifying or so real.

But it isn't your *fault*.

It was the plane.

The impact.

Your head smashing against something, or against a lot of things: the seat in front of you, the ground, Josh Harris. Who knows which blow erased this part of you? Does it matter? Your memory is broken, or rather, you have "limited ability to make new memories," is what the doctor says.

This is who you are now, someone whose thoughts feel like they float away before they can quite stick, before they can take hold. "It may improve," someone said. You don't remember which doctor, or when he said it, but you can imagine his face: grave, serious, and so totally caring, like an actor in a medical drama delivering bad news.

But the doctor wasn't quite right: *Some* things do stick. The important things. Other details slip away as silently as cats in the night.

On the other hand, maybe that's how it is for everyone to some degree. Maybe all of us are holding tight to what we think matters, and releasing everything else into the morass of the past, a hazy place you once visited, taking with you only a handful of glittering stones containing all that you *want* to have matter.

Here is what matters to you: Josh Harris.

The worst part—you don't know if it's connected to your head injury or if your heart just hardened to stone the second that Kath disappeared—is that you didn't grieve. Somewhere inside of you, there is something blocked. It won't allow the tears to come out. If you grieve, it makes it all true.

It makes it all *forever.*

"Kath," you say out loud. Your voice is as dry as crumbs.

"What?" says Josh Harris. "Did you say Kath?"

"No," you answer too quickly. "Duh. I didn't. And you shouldn't either."

He puts his hand on your arm, but you pull it away. Your jaw clenches tightly. He's not allowed to say her name.

No one is.

You know that's unhealthy. You would fix it if you could, throw yourself around the room screaming and crying and pulling at your hair. But part of you can't seem to keep in focus that Kath is dead. It doesn't feel like she is dead. You don't believe it because she still is there. She still talks to you. You know it isn't real but it's real enough.

She isn't *totally* dead, that's the thing.

You kept thinking it would happen, it would sneak up on you, that one day you'd be unable to get out of bed, that you'd be pinned down by sadness, grieving so hard you'd be paralyzed by it. But the sadness flickers at the edge of your vision, never quite becoming full-blown.

It makes you feel terrible, like a monster.

Maybe you *are* a monster now.

But you've been so busy *doing* things—things you've mostly forgotten but which must have happened—like seeing doctors, being fitted with a glass eye. *That* definitely happened, because there it is, in your face. The glass eye is both horrifying and amazing. It's prettier than your real eye and it's not subject to uveitis, which makes it superior in at least one major way, but it is also too cold and too smooth: a marble, not flesh, not *real*. You have to fight the urge you have to tap it with things—a pen, your fingernail—just to feel the solidity of it.

The things you do remember are the first time Josh Harris touched you, a hospital corridor, your stretchers side by side, when he reached out his hand to you. When you were better—or better enough—and going home to California, walking slowly (because everything hurt) between the rows of peach trees, the sun warming your skin, the way he tipped your chin up to his and kissed you.

After Josh Harris started to kiss you, the kissing became everything.

Then, as though it had always been that way, you and Josh Harris were hanging out every day. Every day. Every day.

You are *together*.

You and Josh Harris are Josh-and-Elyse. Elyse-and-Josh.

When reporters started following you around, they shouted questions like, "Why did you live when everyone else died? Do you think you were chosen?" And no matter how many times you said, "We aren't special, it was a fluke," no one stopped asking. Of course they didn't believe Josh Harris wasn't special.

Well, duh.

But he also somehow always said exactly the right thing that made them nod and write things down and then disappear into the blue sky in a way that made you think of Kool-Aid dissolving in water.

Even when it's just the two of you, he still says things like, "While I believe there's a reason for everything, there's no *reason* for what happened to us. We lived because we were sitting in the back row. That's all."

You had offers to appear on reality TV shows. A contract arrived to write a tell-all book. It was exciting. It was terrifying.

You said, "No, no, no, no, no," until you felt like you were made only of that word, screaming through you. "NO." Josh Harris probably felt crazy, too, but he didn't show it. He would never show things like that. Outwardly, he was even, smooth, calm. The whole thing feels now like a dream. You question everything except for Josh Harris and how he was. How he must have been.

Josh Harris is your safe place.

Then something happened and his dad had to sell the bookshop. You frown, struggling to get hold of the memory. A rush of people. A crowd. So many people showing up who didn't want to buy books. Shouting. Wanting. Needing.

They wanted to meet Josh.

They wanted to *touch* Josh.

It was the touching that tipped the balance.

You don't recall how or when it started, or who started it, but rumors and websites cropped up suggesting that you and Josh Harris were saved by God and that God had given both of you the power to heal the sick. You were the Second Coming, the two of you. *You were imbued with God's love.* That was a misquote from Josh Harris in the *People* interview. What he really said was, "I don't know why we lived, but I do know that everyone on that plane was imbued with God's love, alive or dead."

What kind of teenage boy says "imbued"? Only Josh Harris.

To say that the second wave of press was *weird* was an understatement.

You stopped leaving the house. You remember less the reality of it and more the feeling that nothing was safe, nowhere, except for *home*. Everywhere you went, the touchers lurked. Every place on your skin that they touched you, you'd develop real, true hives.

You miss how things used to be simple. But you're also so happy to be here, to be alive, to exist at all. And now you, Elyse Schmidt, are with Josh Harris.

This is why you lived. You're sure of it.

For love.

# 8.

"WAIT HERE, ELYSE Schmidt," says Josh Harris. You blink. Foggy. It's like that for you a lot: like you're looking at everything through a mist.

"Yes," you say. You'd almost forgotten where you were, that he was here, all of it. This keeps happening, this drifting away from yourself and getting tangled up in thoughts and memories. *Blue*, you think. *Tangled up in blue.*

The fog is not blue. It's gray and as dense as smoke. You can almost taste it on your tongue.

Almost.

You try not to dwell on that thought, which is threatening to be confusing. You have to stay in the present or else this happens, this slipping away. You feel the rough grass with your fingers. You break off a piece and hold it under your nose. It smells green and alive.

Josh Harris puts down his beer, which he's been slowly drinking, and leans the bottle against your leg. "Hey! That's cold!" you say. Your voice sounds as though you've been asleep.

"Don't let it spill!" he shouts, getting up in one fluid motion. Then he is jogging across the football field. Considering how much of his body is now made from metal and pins, he still moves like an athlete.

Gorgeous. It's ridiculous really.

You sigh. You're so unbelievably lucky. How did you get so lucky? It's impossible that this is your life now. That Josh Harris is your *boyfriend*.

"Come back!" you call. "Don't leave me here all alone!"

He turns, waving, running in place, like he can't slow down even for a second. "I'll be right back!" he yells. "Don't leave!" Like you would. You grin. Then he's picking something up from the ground and he's sprinting back toward you, clutching a handful of wildflowers, white blue yellow pink purple red, spilling over his closed fist.

"For you!" he says. He's panting so hard he has to bend over, hands on his knees. "Just a second, I have to catch my breath."

You sniff the flowers and sneeze. They are mostly weeds, but they're pretty. "Thanks," you say. Then, "Don't die. Should I call 911? Dude, slow that down."

He flops down next to you. "I'm in terrible shape," he says. "I used to be in such good shape. What happened to me?"

"Um, well, you were in a plane crash and then in a hospital bed for, like, a year?"

"Oh, right," he says. He nudges you, his breathing slowing. "I almost forgot."

"Liar," you whisper, right into his ear.

He shivers. "Come here, Schmidt." He wraps his arms around you and you can feel his heart pounding hard in his chest.

*If only Kath could see me now,* you think. *What would she say?*

*"You two look like photo negatives of each other. I guess it's cool. I'm going to say that it's* striking. *You two are the human equivalent of a double take."*

That's what she'd say.

Maybe.

Definitely.

You can practically hear her voice.

*"It's almost too much. Maybe you should dye your hair so you don't look like a* Vogue *photo shoot gone rogue on the streets of Wyoming. Does Wyoming even have streets? I guess I should say 'on the rugged paths of Wyoming.' This place is terrible. How many people live in this town? A hundred? A thousand? It's like a pimple on the map of America."* It can't be Kath, but there is her voice. In your head, everywhere.

"Kath?" you whisper.

"What?" says Josh Harris.

"Nothing," you say. "Do you like it here? I mean, do you like Wyoming?"

He shrugs. "It's fine. I like not feeling like I'm being followed all over town by someone who just wants me to please touch her sick daughter's forehead to cure her brain tumor.

You know, I didn't mind doing it. It was just too much disappointment to be responsible for, I guess. I totally don't understand how it got so weird so fast, you know?"

"Yeah," you say. "I don't know why I brought it up because I don't really want to talk about it." You have so much more to say that won't come out of your mouth, as though when you try to talk about things like this, your voice becomes too thick to move through the air, the words dropping to the ground before he can hear them. You labor on. "But what if—"

"It *never* worked," he interrupted. "Not once. We'd have heard about it."

"I know, I didn't mean *that*. But I guess it was nice that they thought we could. I wish we could've. But I couldn't touch any more people, either. I don't like *touching*." A bead of sweat has formed on your upper lip. *It's so hard to talk about this*, you want to say, but don't. You wonder if it's the same effort for him, but he's not sweating, not at all.

"You like touching me," he says, grinning. He leans into you, bumping you gently over onto the blanket. Your arms are covered with goose bumps, even though it's hot. The air moves over you slowly like a warm current of water, caressing your hair and your skin. *Sensual*, you think. It's a word you've literally never used before, but there it is.

"I love this," you say, pointing up. The sky is an easier topic. The sky is uncomplicated. "Look. The stars are seriously amazing here. There are way more than at home. Is that even possible? It's like there is a whole other layer of them."

"Yep," he says. "It's very *romantique*." He looks at you and raises his eyebrow, just one, all the way to his hairline. It looks cute but ridiculous, and you laugh, and then he laughs.

"Is that French?" you say. "Are you bilingual now?"

"*Mais oui*," he says. "Aren't you?"

"*Non.*"

"Can I say something that might sound dumb?"

"*Non!*"

"I can't?"

"I'm joking! Of course you can. You can say anything. Duh."

Josh Harris takes a deep breath and lets it out, slowly. "This sky makes me believe in God."

You stop laughing.

"Not me," you say. "I don't. I know you do. That's fine. It's cool. Whatever. But where was God when—"

He holds up his hand. "Everything happens for a reason," he says. "We just don't know what the reason was. For us, I mean, to survive. Not yet. But I feel like we'll figure it out."

"Bullshit," you mutter. "It was random. It didn't have, like, this big *meaning.*"

"I don't believe that," he says.

"You think there was a reason?"

"No. I don't know. Maybe. I guess I think the reason is coming, that we'll figure it out. Eventually. Maybe God doesn't even know yet."

"Well, that's weird. If he's going to pull the strings, he should know why he's pulling them."

"I don't think that's how it works."

"That's because it doesn't make sense, but none of it makes sense. There's no reason or meaning and there's never going to be."

"That's what *you* believe."

"I can't explain it, but I sort of think you sound like an asshole when you say there's a reason. It makes it seem like you think we're special."

"Maybe we are."

"And everyone else wasn't? Yeah, I don't think so."

"Well, I do."

"Jerk."

"I'm not a jerk."

You sigh. "I know. But you say stuff. You told those reporters. I read it in a magazine!"

"I wanted them to stop asking. I didn't want them to ask more *questions*. It seemed like the answer they wanted."

"But do you actually believe we were just better than everyone else? No one was better than—" Your voice catches on the word *Kath*, so you say instead, "—the rest of them."

"We don't have to do this. So let's not, Schmidt," he says, and you know he means, "Let's not talk about the crash," which is fine by you because the effort of it is killing you, even though sometimes it's literally all you can think about, all the time, a scene that inserts itself in front of your every waking moment: Mr. Appleby shouting "HEY!" and the way Kath disappeared and the movie on the tiny screen flickering to black and the yellow oxygen masks dropping abruptly from the ceiling, swinging out of reach, all the blue pushing the smoke and flames away. You can't remember what you had for breakfast or when you bought these shorts, but you remember every detail of *that*.

"Deal," you manage to say, your voice crackling with tears.

*Don't cry*, you tell yourself. *Don't you dare cry.*

A cricket plays a tune with its legs somewhere in the distance, scratching like a tiny out-of-tune violin. Crickets are good luck, your dad has always insisted, because they can only move forward, never backward.

Beyond the cricket, there is the sound of thrumming music from a nearby house, the loud bass rupturing the night into a series of tiny earthquakes. There's a party. It's a party that you were supposed to go to. A wave of young voices rises and falls in a way that makes you think of a volume knob being turned up and down.

You should have gone. Probably. You and Josh Harris, both. How else will you know everyone? How else will you be a part of it? But the truth is, you don't want to be a part of it. You want to be alone with Josh Harris at the back of the plane, alone with Josh Harris on this field in Wyoming, always and forever alone with Josh Harris.

Other people are just too complicated.

Plus, you're going to have to do so much explaining. Of all the things that you imagined for yourself in the future, being someone who has to constantly explain who you are *in terms of a crashing plane* was not one of the possibilities that you'd considered. Josh Harris is the only person you have to explain nothing to, because he was there, which—if you think about it—lines up with your former fantasy of being thrown together by fate.

"This is great," you say. "Way better than that party. Who listens to Guns N' Roses in this century? Is my dad the DJ? I kind of don't think those are our people." You pick up the wilting bouquet. The stems of the flowers are stuck together, gluey with sap. You pull them apart, one by one, and spread the wildflowers around the blanket so that the wind can blow their tangy scent all around you. They smell dry and dusty and remind you of something, a scent memory, but you can't put your finger on it. Your hands feel wet.

The stickiness makes you think of blood.

You sneeze three times in a row.

"Bless you," says Josh Harris.

"I might be *slightly* allergic to these flowers, but they're awesome. Thanks."

"You're welcome," he says. "You're the kind of girl that boys want to pick flowers for, Schmidt."

"Ha." You roll your eyes. "Who talks like that?"

He shrugs. "I guess I do."

Sometimes, like now, you feel like Josh Harris is reading a script but you aren't sure what your next line is, or if your next line matters. Whatever you say, he's going to say the right thing in response.

"Elyse Schmidt," Josh Harris murmurs, and your heart stutters like it always does when he says your name, the

Elyse-part, not the Schmidt-part. You wish he would drop that part. On the other hand, you can't seem to drop the *Harris*.

"Yes, Josh Harris?"

"I thought you might not be awake," he says. "I thought maybe I lulled you to sleep with my gripping conversation."

"Nope, I'm not sleeping. But I've got to say, this World's Greatest Meteor Shower might have been oversold a little. I've been counting, and I'm at . . ." You pause for dramatic effect, and then make a circle shape with your fingers. "Zero meteors. So far."

"I'm also at zero," he admits. "But maybe it doesn't start until later. We could demand a refund. Let's call Ticketmaster." He takes his phone out of his pocket and pretends to dial. This is as close as Josh Harris comes to being funny, so you laugh harder than it warrants.

"*Totally*," you agree. "They owe us front-row seats to something else. We paid good money for this! If by 'good money,' I mean 'nothing.'"

His quieter laugh rumbles through his chest. When it stops, you can hear his heart beating through the thin fabric of his T-shirt. It is so quiet that the wind whistles like a flute through the empty stands.

Neither of you plays the flute anymore.

The flute belongs to a past that doesn't seem real.

You don't even know if there's a band at this tiny high school you're starting at next week, here in Wyoming.

But you know if there is a band here, you won't play in it.

You don't know who you'll be yet, and that thought is so big, it feels as big as the whole night sky, as big and impossible as space itself.

"I wonder what it will be like," you say instead.

Josh Harris shrugs. "It will be like school is always like, just in Wyoming instead of California. It will be the same."

"I guess," you say, but you don't believe it, not for a second. Nothing is the same as it was. Nothing ever will be again.

# 9.

WHEN YOU WANTED to move to Wyoming, your parents laughed at first. You remember that part, the way they looked at each other, confused, like they weren't sure how to respond. In a way, it felt good. It was something they were on the same page about, your craziness. But only briefly before it devolved into fighting about if they would sell the farm, if one of them would stay, if they would move together. And then you begged—you weren't above begging because it mattered so much, in a way you couldn't even articulate— and they'd figured it out somehow, as though you were some kind of puzzle that—if only they could solve you—would make sense.

"Maybe you lived there in your past life," your mom had guessed. "Maybe it's your spiritual home."

"There's no such thing as past lives," your dad said. "That's ridiculous."

"How do you know?" your mom snapped back. "Are you an expert on past lives now?"

"How could anyone know? It's not like anyone actually remembers anything from another life."

"Yes, they do!"

"Oh, sure, on reality TV."

"STOP," you told them. "I just know it's where we *have* to go. I can't explain it. But it's home. Please."

"You probably just saw it in a movie or something," your dad said. "You've never even been there! I've never been there! Neither has your mother! It's a lot to ask, to *move*. And it sounds . . . cold."

You'd shrugged and just kept insisting.

*It matters*, you said over and over again. *I know it matters.*

And it must have worked, because here you are. You *knew* it was the right thing. The only thing: *Wyoming. A pony. Seasons. Snow. Mountains.*

You *convinced* them.

You have a hazy recollection of people walking through the peach farm, with a real estate agent who wobbled alongside them in inappropriately high-heeled shoes. A man with a beard. A woman wearing a kind of suit.

Then there were packing boxes lining the front hall, your dad grumbling the whole time, "Shouldn't we *go* there first? For a vacation? Look around? Just *moving* there seems awfully excessive!"

When you were almost all packed, ready to leave, a man had broken into the farmhouse in the middle of the night and woken you up. You opened your good eye and he was standing next to your bed, mumbling a prayer while he touched your face, his fingers running over your empty eye socket. You didn't scream, instead you took a glass of water from your nightstand and threw it hard against the window. The shattering of the glass was what woke your parents. It was the end of your dad's resistance to the idea. That strange man had really done you a favor, even though he did it in an incredibly creepy (not to mention illegal) way.

You still sort of wonder if he got what he came for, if it *worked*, whatever he was trying to get from you. It's funny how you can't remember so much, but you can remember every detail of his face, the silvery stubble pushing through his skin, the creases around his eyes, the way his hair was wet with sweat.

"I'll be better there," you'd promised. "I'll go back to school. I'll talk to people. I'll make new friends. The *touchers* won't be there. I know they won't. It will be a fresh start. I need this. I need it."

And now you *live* here and you're *Josh Harris's girlfriend* and you have a dog, something your dad would previously have never considered, from a senior dog rescue, a big silky golden retriever named Rumpelstiltskin. He's meant to be a guard dog, but he's not very good at it, not that he's had to be. And you have a pony. Although he's a *horse*, technically. The dividing line between horse and pony is 14.2 hands.

Midi is 14.3, so he's barely a horse, but he's perfect, even though if Kath saw him, she'd say, *"You can't convince people that you aren't a dwarf if you insist on riding a Shetland pony. He makes you look smaller, if that's even possible."* Standing next to Kath, Midnight would look ridiculous, shrunken, but his proportions are perfect and his scale is just right for you. He's a white horse. Whoever named him had a sense of humor. You call him Midi because you don't appreciate it when other people laugh at his name.

Your connection with Midi was what you imagine falling in love at first sight is like—you *recognized* him as soon as you saw him. You knew that you'd just fit together. He looks exactly like the horse you'd always imagined.

And you do fit. You fit perfectly.

You are happy.

*This* is happiness.

You are sure, lying on the blanket, listening to the haunting flute-whistle of the wind, your hand lightly resting on Josh Harris's stomach, that nothing could possibly ever change that.

"The wind sounds like a flute," Josh Harris says, reading your mind.

For a split second, you can see him standing there in Paris, the flute pressed to his lips, his eyes half-closed. You remember the rush of vomit from the wine, the way you had to push past him to get to the potted plant, the way he must have seen you.

What must he have thought?

And then, of course, you can't think about that without thinking about Kath and the past slams into you like the mountain and you disintegrate on contact.

"I'm going to—" you start to say, but then your breath gets tangled in your ribs and your lungs are tatters and it's too late to stop the adrenaline that floods through you so quickly that you can't remember how to breathe anyway, even if it were possible.

In, out, out, in.

*Which way, which way?*

You are gasping, a fish out of water, you slap your hand against your leg, bare in the shorts you don't remember buying, denim shorts, frayed along the bottom, white threads trailing partway down your legs, brushing your skin like insects' legs. *Slap, slap, slap.*

"Schmidt, stop it! Hey! What are you doing?"

You make a humming sound in your throat. Your brain starts to feel heavy and magnetic, like it's being pulled into the ground.

"Schmidt. Hey." He grabs you. Then he is shaking you, your whole body is vibrating. "Breathe. Just breathe."

"I am breathing," you manage to mumble.

You sit up and pull away from him. You suddenly don't want to be touched. You can't be touched. But you also *do* want him to touch you. It's confusing. "I'm fine." You gulp down a few lungfuls of air, hungrily.

"Oh my god. Sorry." You clear your throat, once, twice, three times. You're thinking about frogs. You wish you could stop. That frog couldn't move, pinned in place on the specimen tray. You feel similarly paralyzed. "I don't know what happened." You don't want to cry. You won't. He's staring at you now.

You try again. "I must have just choked on something. Maybe a bug."

"A bug?"

"Just . . . well, forget it. This was supposed to be romantic, remember? World's greatest meteor shower!" You cough again. You can't clear your throat. He looks so worried and so adorable when he's worried and he's worried about you, which is everything, all you ever wanted. You take a long, slow, deep breath.

"Did you know that a meteorite killed a bus driver in India when he was driving? There's no way he went to work that day and even considered the possibility that he might be hit by a shooting star. He got ready for work the same way as always. Packed his lunch. Tied his shoes. Just a normal day. Then a fireball and *bam*."

"Well, no. People don't ever see it coming. We didn't."

"I kind of did, though. I sort of wondered, 'What if it crashes?' Just like I always wondered if I had a brain tumor or Zika virus. I used to have all these pulse apps on my phone and I'd take my pulse about twenty times a day, like it might stop beating if I wasn't paying attention. So maybe I'm not normal, but when I got on the plane, I thought, 'I sure hope we don't crash.' Because crashing on a plane is something that could totally happen. No one expects a meteorite, though!"

"I don't think most people expect the plane crash either. I sort of feel sorry for you! It's like you live every second expecting life to stop soon. That's weird, Schmidt."

"Yeah, well, at least I wasn't *that* surprised when the plane started to fall."

"I was very, very surprised," he says quietly.

You close your eye again. Sometimes it feels impossible to keep it open, like when you're on a roller coaster and you know the big drop is coming and your eyes slam shut in spite of how badly you think you might want to watch this time. Only you aren't on a roller coaster, you're on a field. But even so, the ground is tilting under you, trying to roll you right off the surface of the Earth, trying to pour you up into the sky—*like everyone else*—so maybe you should look, but you can't. You rub at your good eye with your fingers. "OPEN," you command, but it doesn't.

"Schmidt, you should consider thinking less about death and more about life. I do."

*Life.*

*Death.*

*Choose.*

You see a flash of bright blue sky. The front of the plane cleaved off the rear section. Your feet dangling over empty space. It's like you're right *there*. You *are* there. "Josh Harris?" you say.

"Yes?"

"I think I'm having a panic attack." Your voice only comes out in a whisper. "I need an anchor."

You lean forward and press your face into the crook between his shoulder and neck and take in a lungful of his laundry soap, body spray. You touch his smooth scalp, freshly shaved. Your hand is shaking. You open your eyes. You see him. You look at him. Right into his eyes. You stare into Josh Harris's eyes with your one good eye, which you hope isn't red.

*I am the leaf,* you think desperately, because you can't help it.

*I am the leaf I am the leaf I am the leaf.*

You look at the seat next to you and realize that it is empty and that Josh Harris is gone. You unclip your seat belt and make yourself lean forward, like that time you went bungee jumping with Kath and her brothers. They all did these amazing aerial dives that made them appear to be Cirque du Soleil acrobats and all *you* could manage to do was lean and fall, your eyes squeezed shut, anticipating the cord snapping. You once saw on the news someone bungee jumping off a bridge without a cord. The operator had neglected to attach it at the platform so at a certain point in the jump the entire cord passed by the jumper's body. He must have seen it. He must have thought, "Uh-oh." He died, of course.

You lean.

You roll.

You don't die.

# 10.

You are not on a plane. You are on a field in Wyoming with Josh Harris, wildflowers that smell like a memory scattered around you.

You are alive.

You are happy.

"Fuck," you mumble, spinning through space and time.

From far away, you hear Josh Harris say, "Schmidt?"

You put your hand on his arm.

For a while—*After*—your mom tried to tell you to avoid Josh Harris. "You remind each other," she said. "He keeps you stuck there. He's making you anxious."

"No," you'd said. "I need him. He's the only one who understands what it was like! You don't get it. You can't get it. He's my safe place. It's true. Mom. You have to believe me."

"I thought Wyoming was your safe place," she sighed.

"I have more than one safe place!" you said. "It's a metaphor! Or a simile! Or whatever!"

Eventually, somehow, you can't remember how, he won her over.

Josh Harris wins everyone over. And then after his dad sold his bookshop in California, he bought one here in Wyoming, a café-bookstore combination where Josh will work after school, making cappuccinos and charming the shoppers. They live in a house at the end of the same long, gravelly road where you live because Wyoming has no touchers and Wyoming is far enough away to be starting over and Wyoming is safe and somehow even Josh Harris's dad could see the possibilities of Wyoming.

Wyoming is happy, or at least contains the chance of happiness.

It's like you wrote it into being.

Of course, if you'd written it, you would have written that no one else got hurt. That no one *died*.

Wouldn't you have?

You for sure wouldn't have killed Kath.

No one should have died. But they did.

*Everyone* did.

The enormity of that is bigger than anything, a crater left by a meteor, carved out of the ground you are lying on.

You swallow around the lump in your throat. Your breathing has stopped sounding like an asthmatic wheeze, so there's that.

"You okay now?" says Josh Harris.

You nod. You try to think about something else. Anything else.

Somewhere up behind your new house, your dad is thinking of planting Christmas trees. "Why can't you *stop* with the trees?" your mom had asked. "Trees are so much work. Trees take over everything. You don't have time for *us* when there are trees to grow." She clenched her jaw, you could see it working back and forth. "And we don't have to do *anything* right now. We just have to be here for Elyse. We just have to help her find her flame. Be a family."

"Christmas trees are my favorite," you'd said, suddenly wanting to be on your dad's side for a change. "I like Christmas trees. I love them. You should do it. My flame is fine. I'm totally okay."

When you survive a plane crash, it turns out that the airline gives you a check, especially when the plane crashes because the pilot decides he wants to end it all. A really, really big check. No one in your family has to work. Not now. Not ever. All day, every day, the family can sit around the kitchen table, looking at you, waiting for you to figure out how to survive, how to be the Elyse Schmidt with the huge glasses and blue-tipped brown hair who you used to be. The girl with the crooked smile who preferred to draw people instead of talking to them, who imagined a lot more than she lived.

"You *should* plant the trees," you'd said. "Please. Do it. Or get a hobby. Take up quilting. Both of you. *Either* of you.

Take a cooking class. Do *something*. Get a job! God. Anything except all of this *me*."

"But you *are* us," they'd said. "We made you. You are our everything."

"That's too much responsibility," you'd muttered. "Both of you need to get a life." Then you'd stormed out.

You breathe in, hold it, breathe out.

When the people at school—including the kids at that party who are whooping into the night sky—find out who you are, they will tilt their heads slowly to one side, like perplexed puppies. Then their eyes will widen when they recognize you from *People* magazine or even the local news. Even in this small town in Wyoming, it was a big story: two teenagers surviving a plane crash that killed two hundred and sixteen other people on impact. You know it was because you went to the website of the local paper and pulled up the date that it happened, to see if there was some chance that Wyoming was immune from news, a secret pocket of the world that was unreachable by CNN or Reuters or supermarket newsstands or the internet. But of course, it was there. Front page for days and days. Photos of you and Josh Harris, taken from the group band photo shoot, one of his eyes partly closed like he was caught mid-wink, your mouth slightly open like you were talking. A blurry shot of you on a stretcher. A picture of the hospital in France where you were both taken.

And the rows and rows of photos of the dead.

There was a baby! The baby bothers you as much as any of it. The baby and Kath. Everyone else blurs together in your memory: the flight attendants. Mr. Appleby. The Other Max.

There's been a lot of news since: hurricanes and forest fires and bombs in foreign countries, but somehow you know that they will remember. They will know who you are. And they'll stare at you, like they're waiting for you to answer all the unanswerable questions: why it happened, how it happened, why it was you who didn't die. Like *you* have any answers. No one ever wants to hear about how you undid your seat belt and leaned forward. How you rolled down the impossible slope. How the plane exploded. How there wasn't a reason. How no one will ever know, probably. The black box was never found.

You frown.

You think you Googled that but maybe you didn't.

You open your mouth to form the words to ask Josh Harris if he knows but then you realize you don't want to know, you'd rather it was a mystery.

A freak accident.

An unknown, like all good mysteries.

"If we don't see a meteor pretty soon, I'm seriously going to tweet NASA," you say.

"We think alike," he says. "Because I did that earlier. And they just tweeted back! Look." He tilts his phone screen toward you and you read the tweet he's pointing to: "@ FreeThrowJosh00 Here's the secret: You just have to keep looking up."

"Ha ha," you say, even though it isn't really funny. "Sounds like a good life philosophy. Or a future tattoo." You think about it for a second. "Or maybe a poem."

"I'd like it to be a song lyric. It totally works," he says. He picks up his guitar and strums it a few times. "Looking for meteors," he sings. Then he changes it. "Waiting for the stars to fall is like . . ." He stops playing. "What is it like?"

You shrug. "Watching paint dry?"

He makes a face. "That's a terrible line, Schmidt." He strums again. "Waiting for the stars to fall is like falling. Falling in love with a girl, with a girl, with a girl. You just have to, just have to, just have to keep looking up." Strum, strum, strum. "Dramatic finish," he says, then he howls like a wolf into the night.

"Hmmm. Needs work. Too much repetition."

You put your hand on Josh Harris's hand and he covers it with his other hand. You put your other hand on top, and he pulls out his bottom hand and tops yours.

"Are you okay?" he says. "Panic gone?"

You nod. "Yep, all good." You stare into his eyes. Staring into Josh Harris's eyes saves you over and over and over again. Maybe, after all, *he* is the leaf.

The panic subsides, like the slow roll of a retreating tide.

"I'm okay. I'm good. I'm sorry. Let's look up. Always do what NASA says, right? We're probably missing all the good stuff. Meteors crisscrossing the sky like . . . I don't know. Fireflies? Do they have fireflies here?"

He shrugs. "I don't know. Anyway, don't worry about the panic. It happens to me, too, Elyse Schmidt. You don't have to feel bad or be, I don't know . . . embarrassed." He puts his guitar down and smooths out the blanket, then gestures for you to lie down. You take a sip of the bitter, now-warm beer first, then you do. Your breath is going to be terrible, beery and stale.

"I'm not embarrassed."

"Panic is a normal reaction," he says. "To this." He gestures.

"To Wyoming? To the sky? Nuh-uh, I don't think so. Let's not talk about it. Really. It's fine."

"You know what I mean, Schmidt. I get anxious, too."

"I know," you say, but secretly you don't think it's the same thing at all. His panic attacks are so small, you can barely notice them happening. He'll just close his eyes for a second and take a deep steadying breath. It's like a blip. A panic *blip*. A flinch. A few words that he mutters under his breath. *"I do not fear death."*

You shiver.

"I've got you," adds Josh Harris, somewhat pointlessly. "I'm right here."

"I'm fine now, I already said," you snap, but you don't move. "I don't need to be gotten." Josh Harris is sitting up and you sit up and then suddenly, without deciding to do it, you are sitting on him, and he is rocking you back and forth, like a baby. You want him to stop but you also don't want him to stop. Everything is blurry, like a memory of something that is happening at the same time as it *is* happening.

*Ice*, you think. *There was an ice storm. Everything was encased in ice.*

The memory skitters away.

You lose time, that's what happens now. You lose whole scenes, not just from your past, but from your *present*. Your life seems to fast-forward, like you went to the bathroom and missed the main part of the movie and are doomed to be forever confused by a plot twist.

You've started seeing a new doctor, someone who will help you figure out how to manage the blank spaces in your memory. It doesn't matter how big or important an event is, you still seem perfectly capable of having it shimmer in front of you and then permanently vanish, erased for all time.

He is expensive. He is something else your parents fight about, although technically, it is your money.

Another memory or idea or something flashes by you as silver and as quick as a fish.

It's unnerving that ever since you got home, since you woke up, surrounded by cards and stuffed bears, like you'd just been born—*Congratulations, it's a girl!*—you feel like you're only barely hanging on to yourself, clinging by your fingernails to the edge of the cliff, and you have no idea what would happen if you just relaxed and let go.

# 11.

"WHAT ARE YOU thinking about?" says Josh Harris. His lips move against your forehead like the soft touch of wings. You lean into him so they press harder, so you can feel something.

"I'm thinking about nothing," you lie.

"I don't believe you."

"Trying not to be crazy, I guess," you add. "Thinking about not being crazy."

"You aren't crazy."

"Ha, you have no idea." You trace a pattern of freckles on Josh Harris's arm.

The new, expensive doctor—why can't you grasp onto his name?—looks like Dr. McDreamy from *Grey's Anatomy*, a hospital show that your mom watches on old DVDs when she can't sleep, which is often. You don't know how she can stand it, watching that show. People are always *dying*, sick, in pain, or crying. It makes you want to claw out your own ears and eyes—well, *eye*. How is it possible that people can be entertained by *trauma*? Footage of parents flinging themselves down long ER hallways after kids on stretchers . . . Doesn't it *remind* her of what she went through, what she must have gone through?

You can't figure it out.

*How can you* stand *it?* you want to ask.

But it's not just her beloved medical shows; *all* TV shows make you feel unglued. The flash of the images, the bright colors, the laugh tracks—it all makes you dizzy. You can't concentrate on following the stories, and by the time you drag yourself away, your nerves feel frayed and raw.

The news, though, the news is the worst.

The news is *impossible*.

# 12.

"Do you watch the news, like ever?" you ask Josh Harris. "I had to stop watching. I don't know what's happening anymore. Earthquakes or tornadoes or, like, an alien invasion. I have no idea."

"We don't have a TV. You know that. Dad hasn't watched TV since Mom died. We have books."

"Oh," you say. "I forgot. Yeah, actually, maybe I do remember. But wasn't your dad an actor? I remember that he directed the play in fifth grade. What was it? *Our Town*? I guess I thought that actors would like TV. You know, to observe the acting."

"He was a stage actor, so it was different," he says. "Now he doesn't want to watch other people acting. He says it's too hard. He believes there is more to be learned by reading fiction than by following current events. And it freaks him out, watching TV. Falling into a story, being too distracted in case something happens."

"I get it, I think. I haven't watched since . . . you know. But one of us should watch! Or at least Google the news. What if there's a nuclear war or something?"

"The internet is garbage. And we won't need to see it on TV, if it happens," he points out. "We'll all be dead."

"I don't think that's how it works. It's not like everyone *immediately* dies. Some people live and then get sick and die later."

"If there's a nuclear war, I don't think the reporter will be going to work to tell us what is happening. Who would be like, 'Well, got to get to the office and report this!' Everyone would be running for shelter or shooting each other or stealing computers or something."

"Yeah, I guess."

"Or dying. More likely, everyone would be dying."

"Why are you always talking about *dying*?" You are suddenly irrationally irritated. "Stop it."

"You brought it up!" he says. He pushes you gently and you slide off his lap. The ground seems too hard under you, so you stand up. You stretch. You feel strange. Jostled. Shaken up. Like you've just stepped off a ride at the fair and can't quite get your equilibrium.

"I'm sorry," you say. "I'm feeling weird still. Like, not myself." That's the understatement of the year. You *aren't* yourself. You don't even know who yourself is anymore.

He gives you a funny look. "I like to read books more than I like to watch television anyway. The stories stay still."

"Good for you, smarty-pants," you say. "I used to . . . I mean, I still like graphic novels. I think. I haven't read one for a while. But the other books, regular ones, not so much."

"We're different people, Schmidt," he says. "That's what makes this work."

"I know," you say. "I see what you mean about standing still, though. A book is always on hold until you start reading it again. You know what would be sad? If you were reading a really good book and then you died before you finished it. You'd never know how it ended!"

"You could come back as a ghost and read the ending. Maybe we should start reading the last page first, just in case. I guess you never know."

"That's dark, Harris. Even for you."

"I'm not dark. I'm just a realist. People die."

"God, would you *stop*? Where are those stupid meteors?"

You lean away from him and finish your warmish beer, which now tastes like it has absorbed the muggy summer night: You're swallowing the dark blue sky, the humidity, the thick heat of the air. There is something stuck between your teeth that might be a mosquito. You try to subtly spit it out. What if it has Zika? Or worse? You try to think of something clever to say to Josh Harris. Something funny or cute that will make him like you even more but you can't think. You are just so *tired*. You wish you weren't because you want to be enjoying this now-stupid, romantic night. You pinch your wrist, hard. Now is not the right time to fall asleep. You can't sleep at all lately. You think you must lie awake all night, every night, because sometimes—like now—the sleep creeps up on you so suffocatingly that you can barely fend it off.

You hear your mom at night while you are not sleeping, walking around, making tea in the new kitchen. Sometimes, you go downstairs and you find her wrapped in the quilt that grandma sewed when she and dad got married, steam rising from her cup of peppermint tea, the TV volume on low, Dr. McDreamy saving another beautiful patient from certain death. Most times, you don't go downstairs because you can't stand the sight of that show.

Back home—*Before*—you'd have watched it with her, but not now. That would be impossible. You lie awake instead, flat on your back, watching the stars slowly moving past the skylights, watching the sky fade from black to denim to gray to morning, bleached out and too bright, which somehow seems to happen too fast to process, to be too much to absorb.

Coincidentally, *bleached out* and *too bright* is how you look to yourself. By being colorless, you are now extra visible. Blinding. (Like sun on snow or diamonds under a bright jeweler's light.) Your hair, white. Your skin so pale, it's paperlike.

*Be careful what you wish for*, you think, remembering the Swedish band, their pale, bleached, skinny beauty, the way they *wafted*.

You *should* ask your Dr. McDreamy about all of this, about the TV, about the bleaching of you.

You should, but you won't.

Not yet.

How do you ask that kind of question, anyway? You're still on answers. Like, "Um, I don't know." You do a lot of "I guess" and "Maybe."

You can't seem to get Dr. McDreamy's real name to stick in your head. But then again, you've only met him twice. Both times, you were unable to make out most of what he was saying, his voice taking on the soft edges of clouds, drifting around you meaninglessly. But you do remember the chant. He made you repeat it. It was funny because you vaguely remembered it from elementary school, when you used to sometimes have anxiety attacks during tests and you'd faint and have to go to the nurse's office. She'd taught you the same thing: *Touch, listen, see, smell. Anchor yourself and you'll be well.* He even sang it to the same tune.

You wish you'd been able to tell him more, to present him with all that is inside you, the broken parts, so he could fix them. But you couldn't. Still, there was something about him that made you feel reassured, safe, as though if and when you could finally tell him the truth, he'd be able to handle it.

He'd be able to fix it.

You feel the soft plaid blanket. *Touch.*

Josh Harris is playing his guitar again. *Listen.* "Keep playing. That's really good."

"I'm writing it for you," he says. "That's what boys do when they want to win the heart of the girl, right? I'm trying to win your heart."

You laugh so hard that you snort. "Liar!" you say.

He smiles. "I didn't write it," he says. "It's a famous song by the best band in the universe, which, as everyone knows, is the Hoppers."

"The Hoppers are terrible!" you tell him. "I can't believe they still even exist!" Then, "You make their song sound way better than they do. They should thank you." You love the way that you don't have to pretend with Josh Harris anymore. You love the way that you are just yourself: a person who does not like to hear screechy violins.

He strums louder, "Big finish!" he says, which he always says at the end of every song, and then he screams the last line. His voice is swallowed up by the sky, by the grass, by all of Wyoming. You frown. You remember a talent show from before, when he won (he always won) by playing the guitar and finishing this same way.

It may even have been the same song.

You are sure that it was.

"Too much screaming," you say, covering your ears. "Who likes music that screams?"

"Everyone but you, Schmidt," he says. "It's our way of experiencing all of our existential rage about being human without, you know, actually screaming."

"Huh. Well, you *did* actually scream."

"It was a metaphor, Schmidt."

"I don't think that word means what you think it means." You don't remember a time when you've ever laughed this much. *Before,* you were never a person who was just *smiley.*

You were definitely not a person who laughed so much and so often that her stomach hurt.

Right at that moment, someone at the party screams, and then another person.

"See? Existential rage!" Josh Harris says.

At first, you can't tell if the screaming is panic or fun and for a split second, you get that falling feeling that makes you gasp, but then there is the sound of laughter.

Someone applauds.

You put your head on Josh Harris's shoulder. He puts his guitar down and tilts your face to face his own. There is a jagged scar on Josh Harris's perfect cheek. You reach up and trace the scar. It is from *Before*, from something that happened to him as a child. You don't know what it was. It can't have been from the attack on his mother, because he was hiding behind a houseplant. He wasn't hurt. So what was it? You want to ask, but you're almost afraid to know the answer.

Josh Harris doesn't appear to have plane crash scars, which is unimaginable when you think about it, so you try not to think about it. As far as you can tell, even though you know he was in the hospital for as long as you were—he must have been—nothing on his outside reveals anything that happened to him in the crash.

He is unmarked.

You have scars, fine silvery-white threads embroidered into your skin.

Your glass eye is the most visible evidence pointing to the fact that it happened at all. You reach up and touch it. Under your eye, it feels wet, like you're crying without realizing it.

You pull your hand away, quickly. The glass eye is not a scar, it's something different. The sparkling beauty of it makes it seem less like an injury and more like something dreamed of.

"Hey!" he says as you trace his scar up and down. "That feels weird. Stop. Don't stop. Stop. Don't stop."

"Make up your mind!"

"Ummmm, don't stop. Hang on, I'm going to kiss you."

"I won't say *no*."

He kisses you. "Oh, man, I like it when you touch me, Schmidt."

You try to think of the right thing to say back, something pithy and cute. Funny and smart. But what comes out is, "Uh-huh."

"Schmidty, Schmidty, Schmidt." He pulls away from you, so you can see his face, his teeth so white and straight and perfect. "This is better than any party, right? I should have brought romantic food. Frog legs or chicken. Crusty French bread and wine and some very good cheese. And music. A soundtrack!"

"Nah," you say. "Your taste in music sucks. Besides, you're playing a guitar. That's music."

A shooting star carves an arc in the sky above you, leaving a trail of light, a ribbon of blue and red and white light.

"Whoa," says Josh Harris. "Finally. But is *one* really enough to make it the best meteor shower ever seen in the state of Wyoming?" He lifts his bottle of beer and clinks it against your bottle of beer. His is almost empty. Yours is almost full. You frown. You completely remember finishing it.

Didn't you?

This is another complication: Not only do you not remember great swathes of time, things that have happened, but sometimes you misremember what *did* happen.

Maybe that was a different time.

A different night. A different meteor shower.

*Have we been here before?* you want to ask. *Is this a thing we do?* But you can't because then he will not just think you are crazy, he will *know* you are crazy. And then he might pull away. He might stop.

And you don't want this to stop. Not ever.

# 13.

"MAKE A WISH," you say. You are on a blanket on a football field with Josh Harris and it is either the same night or a different night. You look down at your legs to see what you are wearing. Shorts. Are they the same ones? You are suddenly exhausted. A possibility exists that this night is repeating, like *Groundhog Day*.

Would you know if it was?

Does it matter?

You try to smile, make your voice light.

"Come on. Say it with me: Star light, star bright, first star I see tonight, I wish I may, I wish I might, have the wish I wish tonight . . ."

"I think you know what I wish, Schmidt." He leans into you, wrapping his arm around you more tightly, pulling your face into his chest. Everything about his chest is muscular, solid, perfect. You tip your face up toward his and he bends his head toward yours and starts kissing you again

"Velvet," you think. "He has *velvety* lips." You giggle. *Velvety lips.* Like in a romance novel. You can't wait to tell Kath, to hear her laugh and repeat it. Kath's mom was always reading those books. "Bodice rippers." That's what Kath's mom called them. "They're my brain candy."

*"The dead don't really laugh, you know? We just hang out here, in the sky, hoping not to fall."* Kath. Again. *"That's a dead person joke. Really, we're not scared of falling. Why would we be? Already dead, remember?"*

You pull away from Josh Harris, and then flop over on to your stomach, muffling your sob.

"Hey, come back. Are you laughing?"

"I'm right here," you say, facedown, not really answering. The blanket is fleece and somehow smells like chemicals. You think of how when you were walking onto the plane in California, you said to Kath, "It stinks in here!" and she said, "Duh, they have to basically detoxify it between flights so they spray it with *everything* killer. We're probably getting cancer right now, but totally worth it. Paris!" Then she'd high-fived you, but missed and smacked you in the nose instead.

You try to make yourself stop crying. Why are you crying now when you didn't cry before? It's so inexplicable. You breathe deeply (*smell*) and the sob subsides. Then you sneeze. It's strange how the air smells so much like gravel, how dusty it seems. It must be the wildflowers.

"Bless you," says Josh Harris, who is rubbing your back. "You know that people say that because when you sneeze you leave the door open for the devil to come in?"

"Should I let him in? He's probably good company. Anyway, I'm not laughing *at* you! I'm laughing *with* you." Lying comes easily to you now.

"But I'm not laughing."

"You *should* laugh, it must have been funny, whatever it was." *Kath, I'm sorry, it is never funny that you're gone.* "I actually can't even remember what made me laugh."

"Kissing is funny to you, I guess." He makes a face, licks his lips. "I'd like to try again, see if you take it seriously."

"You're funny," you say, pushing him away. "I never knew you were so funny before. Anyway, shhhh. I'm thinking."

"Thinking about granting my wish?"

"Yup."

In the moonlight, the field is silvery. A coyote howls somewhere in the far distance. Or maybe it's a wolf. You're not sure. Are there wolves in Wyoming? You should probably know this. It's always good to know what animals are lurking in the dark.

"This *is* a perfect teen movie, rom-com setting," you say. "I actually am pretty sure I did see this in a movie once." You indicate the blanket and the bag of food and the cooler of beer and then gesture at the sky. "Something more should happen here than panic and hyperventilation, I guess." The howl sounds again. "And possibly a wolf attack."

"You are a perfect girl for one of those rom-coms. I hate those movies, but I don't hate you. Even though you're a hot

101

mess." He flexes his bicep. "I will be your hero! I will protect you from wolves. Or dogs, even. I think that's a dog."

"Emphasis on 'hot,' right?"

"Uh, totally." He laughs. He reaches over and lifts up a hank of your hair and lets it spill over the skin of his arm. It gives you goose bumps, a warm feeling low in your belly.

*"That's not your belly."* Kath, again. *"Don't be juvenile. It's not a secret what happens when you're turned on."*

"God. Shut up," you accidentally say out loud.

"What?"

"I mean, just, how can you hate rom-coms? By their very definition, they are happy, nice stories. They are designed to appeal to pretty much every heterosexual human being. Pretty girl. Handsome boy. A wacky misunderstanding. And then they fall in love. What's to hate?"

"I like it better when there are fast cars or zombies. Remember, Schmidt, I'm a seventeen-year-old boy. So *you* shut up."

Your brain makes the jangling sound it makes when something doesn't fit, a key trying to fit in the wrong keyhole and breaking, loose pieces of metal dropping to the ground. *Clank, clank, clank.* "Seventeen?" you repeat. Your mouth feels funny. Something is wrong. You just can't pinpoint what it is.

"Seventeen," he says. "Did you forget how old we are?"

Your heart is racing.

*Sixteen*, you think. *Sixteen.*

But when you were sixteen, you weren't with Josh Harris. You lived in California on a peach farm. You went to Paris on a band trip.

The plane crashed.

The last year shimmers over the field like a mirage caused by heat.

You lie back down. The stars are still there.

"HEY," says Mr. Appleby, somewhere deep in your brain.

You close your eyes. *"It's all in there,"* Dr. McDreamy murmurs. *"Access your memory files. Your brain is a hard drive."* He is awfully handsome, it's true. He runs his hand through his thick dark hair. *"You just have to find it."* His voice is earnest, kind.

"Okay," you say. "I'll try."

*Click.* There is your fifteenth birthday. There is your cake. There is the party that Kath put on for you, a costume party, roller skates, a cake the size of a table with tie-dyed icing. Kath's face. Everyone is there. Everyone you know. *"Happy birthday, hippie!"*

*"Short-term memory."* Dr. McDreamy's voice cuts through the scene like a sword. *"Head injury,"* he is saying. He sounds so sad, like it's happening to him, personally. He rests his head in his hands. *"Traumatic brain insult."*

*Anchor,* you think. *Or* click through your brain's hard drive. *Which is it? What to do?*

You are on a football field. You are on a blanket. You are with Josh Harris.

*Anchor, anchor, anchor.*

If you can slow everything down, then it's going to be okay. You count to ten, then twenty, then a hundred.

"Schmidt?" Josh Harris says. "Are you freaking out?"

You nod.

"One," he counts for you. He is perfectly patient. Doesn't he ever get tired of this? Of you? (*"Don't be so manic-dramatic,"* Kath says, in your head. *"Dramanic. That should be a word."*) "Two, three, four, five." Josh Harris keeps going and going, his voice low and calm. You focus on his voice and the stars and nothing else. You climb into his voice and pull it around yourself like a blanket. He turns it into a song, strumming the guitar again. "Twelve, thirteen," he sings.

*I am the leaf,* you think. *You are the leaf.*

One of you is definitely the leaf.

"Twenty-nine, thirty, thirty-one." His voice is rushing water, the cooling breeze, the dissipating smoke.

*Click*: You are sitting in a plastic chair. The chair is a murky yellow color. You are singing. Josh Harris is smiling at you. He is in a hospital bed. An operation. He's had surgery on his knee. He blows out the candles on his cake.

*Click*: "Make a wish," someone says. You blow out a single candle jammed into a yellow cupcake. Is it a hospital? You remember nothing of that. Not at all. But in the scene, there is a patch on your eye. You feel relieved. It's fixed! The view out your window was of pine trees, in the far distance, a crashing surf.

*Click*: Josh Harris sloping through the door, ducking to not hit his head. The way he sits in the visitor's chair, his body making a triangle shape with the floor.

*Click, click, click.*

*The files are all there,* you remind yourself. *Just stay calm and look for them.*

*Click*: A lake. You are wearing a bathing suit, floating on a plastic inflatable mattress. The mattress is clear plastic, with rainbow colors underneath.

You blink. Why that mattress? Why now?

"It's just a metaphor," you say. Your voice doesn't quite sound right. "I mean, a memory."

"Okay," Josh Harris says. When he smiles, his eyes crinkle at the corners. The crinkle is everything.

You breathe in and out, slowly. "I was just having, like, a flashback. I guess. Not the crash, but this air mattress. A lake."

"We're both messed up. It's the price we pay for choosing to live." He picks up your hand. He traces your life line with his pointer finger. "Life is complicated. And strange. And then there's death. I do not fear death."

"Don't say that," you say.

"I do not fear death," he says again, and he smiles right at you and kisses you. You taste toast. "I do not fear death," he says, right into your mouth.

"Stop," you say, and you stop his voice with your tongue.

When you both pause for breath, Josh Harris tilts his face up and looks toward the moon. You wish you had a camera to capture it for Instagram, for the world to see how beautiful he is. It makes you gasp. In the moonlight, his face looks like it's been carved out of marble.

"I think you think you're the only one who feels broken. I am, too. I have such bad nightmares. I hardly sleep. I've had them for years, so it's not new, just different." He smiles crookedly. "Ghosts visit me at night, I guess."

"You are too good-looking to be haunted," you tell him. You don't want him to tell you about his dreams. You don't know *why* you don't, you just don't. You want him to stay perfect and to be your safe space. Maybe that's it. You're selfish. You're a terrible person. "Your skin is stone-smooth. Like a granite countertop. If you were a house, you'd be expensive."

"That makes no sense," he says, but he smiles anyway. Who doesn't like being told they are beautiful? His teeth are as white as bone in the moonlight.

"Nice teeth, too," you say. "You could do ads for toothpaste or something."

"Yours aren't so bad either."

"Liar!" you say. You run your tongue around your too-small, slightly gappy teeth. "I need braces."

"Let me look more closely," he says, pretending to examine your mouth. And then he's kissing you again. You feel yourself relax. When he's kissing you, you're fine. You are present. You are yourself.

The sky stretches and sighs above you. Two meteors and then three, then four shoot across it. "Did you see that one?" you say. "Wow."

"Yes," he says. "I see what you see."

You both lie back, hands entangled. You search for something to say. It was easier when you drew it, when you filled in both your speech bubble *and* his. In real life, he sometimes says things that you don't know how to respond to exactly, so you let them sit there, unanswered. In real life, you blurt dumb things. "You're a really good kisser."

"Thank you."

He is sometimes so polite that his politeness is almost rude. His manners are also his armor that prevents you from getting too close to his heart.

*"Terrible, Schmidt,"* says Kath. *"That's like the most sophomoric poetry I've ever heard. Never say that out loud. Hard eye roll. Hey, can you roll a glass eye? Asking for a friend."*

"Stop," you try to say, but nothing comes out.

*"You fetishize manners. Have you ever thought of that? You always like those English actors. And they might be rude as anything, but the accent gives the illusion of properness. Right? And Josh is kinda strange with the way he talks. Like he's onstage. Like he's EEE-NUN-SEEE-ATE-ING. I'm just saying, there's something off about your taste, Nerdball."*

You press your fingers into your ears but you can still hear her and you don't really want to block her out at all, so you take your fingers out again and press your arm over your mouth and into your sleeve and you whisper, "Sorry, sorry, sorry." A whole slurry of sorries, but Kath can't hear you. Obviously.

Kath is dead.

"Kath is dead," you say, but Josh Harris is playing his guitar again and he misses what you said, which is lucky, because then he doesn't have to respond.

# 14.

"Ahhhh, did I just see another one?"

"No. I mean, maybe. But I missed that one."

Your white hair is spreading all around you on the plaid blanket (*also Instagram-worthy*, you think), your arm over your good eye. You move your arm so you can see the sky. There *are* more stars in Wyoming than there were at home. You wish the party music would be turned down, the ongoing drone of the bass keeps vibrating through you, there's a squeak of strings, people laughing too loud. The party you were *supposed* to go to. The one where all the kids who will be at your high school are drinking and getting high. You can't imagine how that would have gone if you'd just showed up at some stranger's house with a six-pack of Heineken.

Suddenly, you feel confused, like you've missed a step and are falling down the stairs: Why *are* you here in Wyoming? How is this going to go?

"Are you going to play football? When we start back to school?" It's not really what you mean to ask. What you want to ask is, *Are you going to be normal? Blend in? How do we do this?*

*Normal.*

What does it even mean?

Josh Harris shrugs, which you can feel more than see. "I'm not that interested in sports anymore. They don't feel important to me. Also, there's my knee. Sports are like something for people who never have anything to worry about. But maybe basketball. I still love basketball. Do they even play basketball in Wyoming?" He shoots a fake hoop. "I miss basketball and Fitzy."

"Yeah," you say. You clear your throat. "I get it."

"What do you miss, Elyse Schmidt?" he says.

You think about it:

You don't miss anything.

Do you?

*"You miss me, you jerk. Duh."*

"Obviously," you mutter.

You miss having an unrequited crush on Josh Harris. Having a requited crush is better and worse at the same time. *Paradox,* you think. *Or something like that.* Instead of being your background music, now he's your full symphony. But you have to be his, too, and you don't quite feel like enough somehow.

"I miss being able to see out of my right eye," you say, finally. You can't seem to say Kath's name but you know that she knows. She has to know.

"Yes," he says. "I can *see* that." He grins. "Do you see what I did there?"

"Ha ha," you say. "You're hilarious."

"I hope *you* think so." He nudges you. "Girls like funny guys. I've heard that." His laughter rolls around him, doughy and stretchy, a loaf of unbaked bread. You are struggling to picture him having a conversation with Danika Prefontaine, ever, much less being in a relationship with her. He's so peculiar. The way he talks. Kath is right. Something is off. Not in a *bad* way. *You* like peculiar, so that's fine. You can relate to peculiar. But you can't understand how *she* did. No one is more normal than Danika Prefontaine. Well, *was*.

Now she's dead, just like all the others.

"*Dead is the new normal. Dead is all the rage. Everyone is doing it.*"

"Kath," you blurt. "I miss Kath. It's crazy how much I miss her."

"I know."

"You don't, though. You can't know."

"Why not? I miss Fitzy."

"You were 'buddies,' it was different."

"You think that your friendship with Kath was better because you are girls?"

"I know that sounded terrible. I'm sorry. I'm a jerk. Just because I survived a plane crash doesn't mean I'm a good person. I should warn you right now that I don't think I really am a good person, actually. I just gave you evidence. I *get* that you miss Fitzy. Of course, you do. I'm just . . . I guess everyone thinks what they have is more intense or better than what everyone else has."

He stares at you, unblinking. "Maybe I'm not good either," he says.

"Ha! You're Josh Harris. Trust me, you're good."

"Why do you think that? You don't know what I think about most of the time. You don't know. You just think I'm good because my mom died and that seems heroic to you, but I was just *hiding.* I wasn't a hero."

"That's not true," you lie, even though it is. "I don't think that."

"I can be an *asshole*, too, you know," he says.

"You never even use that word! When you say it, it sounds weird. Like you're talking in a foreign language or something!"

"Asshole," he says again, raising his eyebrows.

"See?"

"It's not a comfortable word for me," he admits.

"Exactly. Ha. That's because you're a good person," you say. You pretend to write it down. "I'm putting that into evidence."

"No, it's because my dad would kill me for saying it," he says. "It's really important to him. He has this thing about rising above. He rises above by talking in a certain way. It's hard to explain." He laughs. "He likes it when I read Shakespeare out loud after dinner. And it's okay. It's like he needs it. It's fine. I don't mind doing it. I used to think kids would think I was a freak, but mostly they don't say anything. Maybe they don't notice."

*"Yeah, right, they don't notice. What a dreamer. Everyone notices! It's weird, Elyse. It's like showing off. Rise above, my ass. He just sounds pompous. I don't know why you're so into him. He's not so special, he just thinks he is."*

You swallow around the lump in your throat. "I think you're special," you say. "I mean, I like it. It makes you sound sophisticated, I guess. And there's nothing wrong with being different."

"But it's my dad's idea, not mine. It's his idea of who I should be. I sometimes feel like we're all playing a part on a show that we didn't sign up for. Maybe we did. I'm not allowed to watch television so maybe this is actually a reality program and we don't know we're on it and it's all some kind of a test."

"There was a movie like that. I think Jim Carrey was in it. It was messed up. But even then, no one would fake a plane crash. That would be impossible. So we can probably pretty much rule that out."

"I never saw that movie."

"You need to watch more movies that aren't just one long car chase. Broaden your horizons, dude!"

He shrugs. "I'm reading all the books my dad tells me are classics. He says they are important. They're pretty boring. But . . . I don't know. I guess reading them makes me feel like a better person."

"Heavy," you say.

"Well, some of them are so boring that I'd rather be engulfed by flames than have to read them," he says. "Does reading boring books make you a better person?" He pauses, scratches his shoulder. "I always tell my dad that I think they're great."

"Well, look, there is nothing good on TV anyway."

"What do you do at night?"

You shrug. "I . . ." You frown. "I was going to say that I draw but I guess I don't do that much now. I think I . . . Well, I go for rides. When I'm in the house, I just . . . I don't really know. I lie on my bed. I look at stars through the skylight. I try to remember things. I think."

"You don't *know*?"

"Duh, of course I know. I don't read classic literature, but for sure that's a better answer." You mock-punch him in the arm. "I guess I'm not as good a person as you are, Saint Josh."

"Ha ha, you're very funny."

You laugh, to show him you know he's kidding around, or this is as close as he gets to it. Then you choose your next words carefully. "I still think you're inherently good, even if you do have all this pressure because your dad has such specific ideas about what's good and what's bad. I mean, some teenagers would take one look at 'classic literature' and totally refuse, but you love your dad—even if he's super weird—and you don't want to disappoint him." You mime a check mark. "Check. Good person points."

He doesn't answer right away. "Thank you, Elyse Schmidt," he says.

"You're welcome, Josh Harris," you say.

"I think you're a good person, too," he says.

"Yeah, well, you're wrong. I'm not. I don't know what I am. I won't even watch my parents' stupid TV shows with them and I sure wouldn't read for my own good, or whatever. And I'm not always thinking nice things. I'm not always like, 'Yes, ma'am, you can touch my arm on the off chance that it cures your incurable cancer!' If I were a good person, I'd let people rub my whole body if it could fix whatever is broken about them. Think about it. If there was someone you could touch who could fix all your broken parts, would you touch them? I totally would. Which makes me a hypocrite."

"I'd like to touch your whole body," he says, raising that one eyebrow again. "You can cure my broken parts."

"Ugh," you say. "You're right. You're not a good person. You're a boy, being led around by your penis."

He laughs. "Sorry," he says. He doesn't sound sorry.

"Jerk," you say.

He laughs again.

"You won't even fight with me. Why don't you ever want to fight?" You hit his arm again, this time less gently. "Pow, pow."

"I'm not a fighter," he says, simply. "Life's too short for that." He pushes himself up on his elbows. He lowers his forehead to yours and stares into your eyes until you are dizzy. His eyes are blacker than the sky. Unbroken by stars, falling or otherwise.

"Kiss me already," you say. "You good person, you. Whisper me the plot of *War and Peace* or something."

Josh Harris kisses you in a way that erases the field and the music and the crickets and the stars, which aren't falling, and the plane that crashed in the mountains in France one long year ago. "It's about war," he whispers. "I'm guessing the end will bring peace. A boy is in love with a girl, but she is unfaithful. He'll forgive her, I think. It's . . ." He concentrates on kissing you for a minute. "It's really boring."

"Stop," you say. "I'm already bored. Let's stick with kissing."

Josh Harris kisses you and kisses you and kisses you. The thing with being kissed like that is that you become nothing more than a body, another human body, under this huge net of stars. And it's so easy to be just a body.

It's getting to be so easy to be *you-and-Josh-Harris*.

# 15.

YOUR BEDROOM IN your new house is exactly the dream room
you imagined for most of your childhood. It is storybook
perfect. It is the whole top floor of a century-old house that
has been painstakingly remodeled to feel both fresh and new,
and like something from a museum. The room itself is a
converted attic with sloping ceilings. Everything is painted
white. You have your own bathroom attached, with a black-
and-white tile floor and skylights and huge green plants that
hang from hooks in the ceiling, spilling their rich greenery
everywhere, chlorophylling the air, which smells like the air
in a greenhouse, extra-oxygenated and scrubbed clean by the
leaves, so many leaves.

You have skylights above your bed, too, so that you can lie
in bed and see the stars. You can open them up and the night
air rushes in through the cracks and it's like being outside

without being outside. You have a closet with a secret door in the back and beyond that door, a tiny room with a round window. You've set up a reading nook, piled with your favorite graphic novels for inspiration and big pillows that would make an ideal place to sit to draw your own comics and to think about Josh Harris. You have a desk in there where you keep your favorite drawing pens in mason jars, waiting for you to want to draw again. You *will*, one day. Eventually. You're sure of it. You just haven't been able to, since *Before*. On the other hand, maybe Josh Harris was the only story you had to tell and now that he's your reality, you've got no need for an imaginary existence.

In your drawer, you have some old sketchpads. *WEIRD WAYS TO DIE* is your favorite one, but also *SELFIE DEATHS*, which is one hundred panels you drew inspired by internet stories about people who died taking selfies. Climbing onto train cars to take a pic of yourself and being electrocuted is a surprisingly common way to die. Who knew? (You're getting good at drawing trains.) Another common one is accidentally shooting yourself in the face while pretending to shoot yourself in the face. The moral of that story is pretty obvious but people are dumb so you guess as long as there are train cars to climb on and guns to point at yourself, people will keep doing it, and keep dying.

You're definitely not inspired to draw people dying anymore. What kind of crappy person draws something like that?

Over the window in your reading nook, you have hung the peach silk scarf that you bought in Paris. Someone—your mom, you suppose—must have cleaned it and mended the tears with tiny stitches done by hand. You can't even see them unless you look super closely, and even then, like the scars on your body, you have to know exactly where to look. That dumb "sophisticated" scarf and those nearly invisible stitches torture you. You don't want to remember but they make you remember and then you do want to remember and then you think, *Kath*. You run your fingers over the material again and again, compulsively, when you see it. It's so impossibly smooth and perfect, but now there are the bumps of the threads, reminding you and reminding you.

You don't know what you were thinking, buying that thing. You will never be a sophisticated, scarf-wearing Parisian. You are a person who is dwarfed by your glasses and can't figure out how to get your brows to look like something fashionable, like everyone else's. You like to wear T-shirts featuring animals with mustaches.

You are *not* a sophisticate.

You are not Kath.

When the sun shines through the peach pattern, you can remember exactly the day you bought it, the way Kath laughed at you (*"Peaches are the bane of your existence! Remember? Why are you buying peaches?"*), the way the man took your money pityingly, knowing the scarf was too nice and too expensive and all wrong for the likes of you.

You weren't happy then.

Now you are happy.

But Kath is *dead*.

Everyone is *dead*.

Your life is completely different at the cost of two hundred and sixteen lives.

How dare you even think about being happy?

You hate yourself.

You also don't know how to stop that thought from looping.

*I am happy.*

*Kath is dead.*

It's better not to think about it. It's better just to *be*, to not worry about gluing the scenes of your life together, to just be present in them, to just be happy.

*I'm doing it for you, Kath*, you think, but even you don't believe that.

You're doing it for yourself.

*Asshole.*

You were in your new room in your new house with your new boyfriend, Josh Harris, when the earthquake struck.

At first, you weren't sure what the sound was. You were deep in a strange web of awkwardness that came with showing your new *boyfriend* your new *bedroom* while both of you pretended to not be looking right at the bed, thinking things to do with sex and beds and possibilities. The roar sounded like a truck backing up, the sound becoming a feeling that rumbled through the house, vibrating pictures off the wall. Then one louder bang and the walls undulated, the floor tilted, you slid into Josh Harris and Josh Harris caught you and said, "I think something's happening."

"Uh, yeah," you said. "There are canned goods in the basement."

It was the first time you made him laugh. He wrapped his arms around you and you felt that laugh, the vibrations rounder and more musical than any kind of laugh you'd heard before. "I'm not hungry, Schmidt," he said. "Maybe we should wait to see if we'll be trapped here forever before we start eating the ravioli."

"Are you okay up there?" your mom called. Rumpelstiltskin started barking. Josh Harris and you fell backward onto the bed, still laughing, still vibrating, still holding on to each other, and then kissing and kissing and laughing and his hands started going to the places where boy's hands go when you are kissing like that and you stopped laughing, but you only let his hands go to so many places before you said, "Stop."

And he did.

# 16.

"I'M STUPIDLY HAPPY," you whisper, on the blanket, in the field, when Josh Harris pulls away, when he stops kissing you and you stop kissing him back, just for now.

"Good. I'm happy, too. But should we have gone to the party? The first day of school's going to be strange. Everyone will stare at us. We won't know anyone."

"You're used to being stared at!" you remind him. "People stared at us at home, too. People stare. People are stupid. Half the time they're staring because they're racist dicks and they're like, 'Oooh, a white girl with a black guy.' The other half, it's because we're *the ones who lived* and they can't figure out why we're so special and then somehow in their head, they start thinking, 'They think they're so special!' and then they hate us. Because: Dicks. Or, you know,

they want something from us. *Power.* Like we have power?"
You pause. "They all want us to be either gods or freaks.
Those are pretty high expectations."

"Maybe," he says. "It's funny to hear you say that word."

"Which word? Gods? Freaks?"

"Ha ha, no. Dicks."

"Dicks!" You start laughing. "Dicks dicks dicks."

He cringes. "I wouldn't've expected that. I don't know,
Elyse Schmidt. You were always so quiet. You were always
the good girl in the front row. I thought . . . I thought, 'She's
like me.' I knew we were so different and that you'd never be
interested in me, but on the inside, I'm . . ."

You giggle. "On the inside, you're a quiet, smart girl?"

He smiles. "Yeah, that's it. Basically."

"I'm still quiet," you point out. "I sat in the front because
my eyes are bad. Anyway, you didn't like me. You had
Danika. You had *everyone*." You want so badly for him to say
that Danika was a nightmare, then you hate yourself, because
Danika is dead. You stretch your legs out so hard that your
calf cramps, which feels right, like what you deserve.

"Danika," he repeats, quietly.

"Forget it," you say. "Forget I mentioned her."

"You didn't like her?"

"I hate people. Other than you. And Kath." You close
your eyes and it's like she's still there, in front of you. *"You
know, I was thinking . . ."*

"That's sad. I like people. I think people are mostly good,
or at least okay. On the inside."

You groan. "Yeah, for some people, they keep that really deep inside, tucked in behind all the douchiness that they wear on the outside."

"Douche armor," he says, making a face. "I think you're wrong. You see what you want to see. I want to think everyone is good."

"Well, you're wrong," you tell him, sticking out your tongue.

He lightly punches your leg. "Pow, pow. Don't make me fight with you, Schmidt."

"As if you would." You roll away. "I feel bad for feeling happy. Do you think it was just dumb luck that we didn't die?"

"I think it was *weird* luck. Sometimes I think it was good luck. Sometimes I think it was bad luck."

"Bad luck?"

"Yeah. Because by living, now we owe something. We owe the people who died something. We owe everyone everything." He closes his eyes. "We have to be grateful all the time."

"Or else what?"

He opens his eyes and looks at you. "I don't know! It just feels like this pressure, when really, no one probably expects anything from us, at all."

"Right, that's why people back home were always grabbing at our clothes so we could fix everything that was wrong with them. What about what's wrong with us?"

"I think that was a really small group of people. It just felt like a lot. Most people probably don't think about us at all."

"Do so." You stick out your tongue.

"Uh-uh," he says. He stretches so far that his arms and legs reach off the sides of the blanket. He fans them up and down, like he's making a snow angel. He yawns. His tongue is covered with those small velvety bumps that remind you of something. You smell toast and laundry detergent and suddenly you feel so sleepy.

"Pith," you say.

"What?" he says.

"Nothing!" you say. "I don't know why I said that."

"I thought you said Kath," he said. "I thought you said her name."

"Well, I didn't," you snap.

A meteor streaks through the blackness, cleaving the night sky into two halves, leaving a tail of vibrant blue then yellow then white, like a firework on the Fourth of July.

"Wow," you say.

"What's *wow*?"

"You missed one! Open your eyes."

"They're open now."

"Okay, good. Keep them open and wait."

You lie quietly beside each other, breathing, your leg touching his leg, your side touching his side. You should do something, you think. But what? Other girls would know what to do, lying on a blanket with Josh Harris. Danika would, for sure. Other girls would probably be having sex with him by now. You put your hand on his leg but it feels wrong, like it's at the wrong angle or your arm doesn't belong to you, so you jerk it away.

You are just so *awkward.*

"Look! Another one!"

"Missed it," you say.

"Keep your eyes open." He grabs your hand, hard. It hurts until he relaxes his grip a bit. Your heart is racing.

Another meteor races across the sky.

Then another and another, like God has thrown a handful of them all at once, a sparkler bouquet.

"Close your eyes! Make a wish! Make a hundred wishes!"

"I wish," he says. He lets go of your hand and leans up on one elbow. He stares at you unblinking. "Wishes aren't something I usually make, but if I did, you would know what I wish for."

"Oh." You try to keep your eyes on his face, but it's almost shimmering. Josh Harris is asking you for sex. You smile a little, but then the nervousness comes back, wrapping around your neck like a hand. You clear your throat. "Your *wish.*"

Josh Harris wants to have sex with you, which is mindboggling, in and of itself! You'd be crazy not to do it! But.

But.

The thing is that you're just not sure that you're *ready.*

*"It's not an* exam. *You don't have to prepare. Besides, everyone knows the first time is terrible. It's supposed to be so that when it gets good, it's even better than good because it's unexpected. Like if your parents forgot your birthday one year, and then they remembered the next year, the next year would be so great, right? Don't overthink it, Schmidt. It's basically just a bad birthday. Think about it."*

"I *know.* God."

"What? Are you mad?"

"Nothing! I wasn't talking to you. I was just . . . I was thinking out loud."

Josh Harris reaches out and tucks your hair behind your ear and you kind of want to die because if you die right now, in this second, at least you're dying *happy* and in love.

"Loved," you whisper.

"I really can't hear you," he says. "I think there must be something wrong with my ears. Sometimes it's like there is a roar that only I can hear."

"That's because you're a weirdo," you say. You reach up and touch your hair in the same way that he just did. You tuck it behind your ear again and again. "Or, you know, because you had a head injury?"

"You're the one who had the head injury," he points out. "My leg. Your head."

"Oh, right. I'm forgetful," you say. Your heart feels rubbery. You think about a game you used to play with Kath at school recess, when you were in third grade. You had these rubber balls, special ones, and they were tiny and bounced high. There was a game, Seven Up maybe? You had to throw the ball in a pattern against the wall. One bounce, two bounces, no bounces, clapping in between. You've forgotten some of them, but suddenly you're there, on the playground, the familiar bumpy pavement under your feet, the brick wall with one off-color brick that you'd get bonus points for hitting, Kath turning cartwheels behind you, the smell of rain evaporating off the ground in steamy waves.

The sun is in your eyes and it hurts. You blink.

"Are you crying?"

"The sun is in my eyes!"

Josh Harris sits up straight. "It's night now," he says, so quietly that you almost wonder if he said anything at all.

"Duh," you retort. The ground tilts and tips. It's your ear, that's all. An inner-ear thing from the crash that you can't shake that sometimes spins you around.

"If you could time travel . . ." you start, but you let it trail off.

"I'd save my mom," he says quickly, right away, like it would be bad luck not to say it. "But we can't change anything. We can't change what happened to her or to us." He traces something with his finger in the sky. "Big Dipper," he says.

"I can never see which constellation is which," you say. "It's all just disconnected dots. Like the stars are strangers." You feel like you're stalling, because you are stalling. You knew this was going to happen tonight, but you sort of didn't believe this was *actually* going to happen tonight, and you aren't ready for it to happen tonight while at the same time you desperately want it to happen tonight. You clench your jaw so tightly, it hurts.

It might happen.

It might not.

It's up to you.

You get to *decide*.

But there is no decision.

"It's going to happen," you whisper. You *intend* for it to sound sexy, but your voice is shaking. In the distance, a car slams on its brakes and the squeal of tires rips through you like a blade. You take a breath and you lean up and over and you kiss him. You kiss Josh Harris. You've forgotten how to move your lips, but you're trying. You are trying too hard. You can feel your effort. It's making you sweat. Why is it so hard to not be awkward? You'll never understand. Kath would have been naked already.

*"Just take off your stupid clothes and jump him. Don't make everything into an impossible equation to solve. Life isn't calculus. Be Nike: Just do it."*

You keep kissing him with your eyes open so you can see his face.

He opens his eyes and he is looking at you, too, but he's not exactly kissing you back. He's being kissed, which is not the same thing. His eyes are mirrors and doors and windows and everything to his soul and your soul, and he says, his lips touching yours, "Are you totally sure, Schmidt?"

You breathe him in and you say, too loudly, "Yes."

The next meteor's tail fades back into blackness, the stars keep falling, shining, watching, staring, judging how happy you are.

*Are you happy now?*

*Are you still happy?*

*Are you happy enough for all of us?*

*If we had lived, we would have been happy.*

*We would have done everything.*

*You have to do everything.*

*For us.*

*Because you lived.*

*You have to do it for us.*

*You are us.*

*We are you.*

*You are the everything.*

*We are watching, watching, watching, wanting.*

Josh Harris is pulling at your clothes, untying your halter. You feel the night air on your skin, which is abruptly bare. Your nipples tighten. You fight the urge to cross your arms over your chest, to hide your breasts, which are too white in the darkness. And now his breath is catching and so is yours. Then you are moving again, you are pulling at his clothes and he's stuck in his shirt and laughing, but you aren't laughing, you need to get your skin to touch his skin, to remove the night air from between you, to make no space between you. Then he's free of the shirt and twisting out of his pants and your shorts are gone, too, and you don't know how to cover all the parts you suddenly want to cover and you can't stop staring at his penis. You've never seen a penis before. You feel yourself starting to hyperventilate. You would rather die than faint right now, but you might faint. It's complicated.

"I . . ." You start to say something, but you don't know what it is.

And then he is tracing his fingers over you, over all of you, and you are letting him do that, you are trying not to be scared, and then he is kissing you again and just like that, in an instant, everything is perfect and you aren't scared.

*Not even a bit*, you think.

(*"You're a terrible liar,"* says Kath. *"But it's pretty normal to be scared. Just try not to think about anything. Try to just feel."*)

"Since when are you a sexpert?" you say. "You didn't even . . ."

"What?" says Josh Harris, stopping what he is doing with his hand, which is a relief but also you don't want him to stop.

"Stop, go," you say.

"Are you okay, Schmidt?" he asks.

"Yes." You close your eyes. "Yes. I mean it, yes. Really."

"Yes?"

"Yes."

And then you don't have to think about anything at all, you just have to *feel* (Kath is right), at least for now. Then you are on your back and he is inside you, it happens so fast, and it is such a jarring pain. It hurts! You didn't know, but you did. Then it's over, but even though it's over—the part that hurts—a tear rolls down your cheek, which you quickly wipe away so he doesn't ask you why. Then it stops hurting or you stop caring and you just don't want him to stop, not now, not ever.

Over Josh Harris's shoulder, you see another shooting star and then another, like fireworks, like applause.

It *is* the best meteor shower in history, after all.

In the distance, someone is *yahoo*ing. A dog is barking. A siren wails. Something clatters. Someone shouts. An owl answers the siren's call. The dog's bark turns to a howl.

There's just so much noise, it's hard to separate out what each thing is, just a jumble of volume that goes up and down and then stops.

It's quiet.

The unnaturally green field is holding you up and your bodies are doing what bodies, it turns out, just *know* how to do. *("See? Press a couple of bodies together, and presto!")*

"Presto," you mumble. Your body is moving of its own accord. It's nothing to do with you and everything to do with you.

"You," mumbles Josh Harris, into your hair. "You."

"You, too," you whisper, not quite knowing what he means, but hoping.

It is still so warm and the stars are patterning themselves into new shapes over Josh Harris's shoulder that you'd draw, if you still did that kind of thing. You would. You'd draw new constellations. You'd draw colors that can't exist.

And then it stops.

It's over.

It was everything and it was *light* in a way you can't explain and the blanket is damp with your sweat and you can't wait to tell Kath all of it, everything.

You cough. *Ribbit, ribbit.* A frog in your throat. "Do you still think we should have gone to the party? Met some new people? Blended in? Practiced normalcy?" Your voice sounds too loud in the stillness.

"Elyse Schmidt," he says. "Oh my god. You know what? I think I love you."

You give that a minute to sink in, time to leave a mark, etched permanently into you. "Josh Harris," you say. It's all you can say.

Stars flee across the sky, one after another, either trying to get away from you or to come closer. You don't have to make a wish because all your wishes have already come true.

Or almost all of them.

# 17.

It's THREE IN the morning and the front door squeaks when you open it, the screen banging behind you, but no one calls out, no one stirs.

Your parents are asleep. Rumpelstiltskin, the golden retriever you forgot that you had, looks up from his position on the living room couch, blinks sleepily, thumps his tail, and then puts his head back on his paws and sighs. You go over and plant a kiss on his soft, old head.

"I had sex with Josh Harris!" you whisper. You want to say it out loud so you don't forget that it happened, so you can hold on to it. So much of what has happened *After* has just slipped away from your grasp. "Rumpelstiltskin," you say, to remind yourself of his name. The dog opens one eye and stares at you, blinking in the light. "What?" you say. "It was very romantic. Trust me." He sighs, a long half-snore burbling from his throat. "Be that way then," you tell him. "You're a terrible guard dog."

You take the stairs two at a time. There's an energy coursing through you. You almost wish a car would fall on someone so you could use this strength to lift it off. If you were on a crashing plane right now, you'd be able to stop it with your mind. The air is solid and moves like something silk wafting around you, like everything that happened, like everything that *is* happening.

The windows are open in your bedroom. The curtains are lifted by the breeze and then gently sink back into place, pooling slightly on the wood floor. The room is full of the night: velvety darkness, pinpricks of light. You collapse onto your perfectly made bed and the sheets are cool, smooth, soft, tucked tight.

"I slept with Josh Harris!" you tell Orange Rabbit, perched as he always is on the shelf next to your bed. His head leans too far to one side. "This is *love*. I'm in love! He said he loved me. It's all I've ever wanted. And now I have it." You consider this while you try to straighten his head, but the stuffing is too loose in his neck to support it. It falls forward. "Well, he said, 'I think I love you, Schmidt.' It was close enough." You hesitate. "Right?"

You pick up your iPhone from beside Orange Rabbit, knocking him onto the floor. You reach down and pick him up. You press him to your nose. He smells like sleep and something else, something like your entire childhood, like everything that's ever happened to you. You tuck him under your chin.

It's 3:14 a.m. *Pi o'clock*, Kath would say. She loves math.

*Loved* math.

Past tense.

"Kath loved math," you say out loud, feeling the rhyme click together. "Elyse loves Josh Harris."

*"Is that a poem? It doesn't rhyme. That's awful, if it's supposed to be verse."*

"Only the first part," you say. "Nothing rhymes with Elyse except fleece." Fleece is terrible for the oceans, you remember. Something about how it breaks down in the washing machine, filling the ocean with plastic bits. "Elyse hates fleece," you say, out loud.

The room around you is so still, it feels almost painful.

"Kath?" you say.

You turn on your phone and you dial her number. You let it ring and ring and ring and ring. "Hey, it's me, Kath, sing me a message, damn it."

"Hey," you say, your voice cracking. "Happy pi o'clock." But it's not pi o'clock in Cali, it's 2:14. "I mean, Happy pi o'clock in an hour," you amend. "I don't sing, but guess what? We did it! Me and Josh Harris. It wasn't terrible. You were wrong. It was perfect, everything was perfect." You pause for a beat, the beat that you hold open for her to reply. "Kath? It did hurt a little. It passed really quickly. The pain part, I mean. After it stopped hurting, it was easy. I didn't have to think about it."

Nothing.

You forge ahead. "Anyway, there were *literal* shooting stars. Not a metaphor. When does that ever happen? It was like a movie or a book or something." You wait another beat. Still nothing. "And don't worry, we used something. We aren't going to be a cautionary tale." *Beat.* "And Kath? He said he loves me. Josh Harris! Said that! To me! It's like, I don't know, it's a *miracle.*" *Beat.* "I mean, maybe that's a waste of a miracle, if you think about all the things that miracles should have been used for. I'm sorry. I'm an asshole. I shouldn't have said that. Erase that bit about the miracle. But anyway." *Beat.* "I'm the happiest girl alive. Call me?" *Beat.* "Love you. I miss your face."

You tap the red button on the phone and open up the text screen, reading through your last few texts from Kath. "Stop calling him JoshHarris! His name is Josh! Just Josh." "Related: Why does he call you Schmidt? So unsexy, Nerdball." "Unrelated: Max says that he likes tall girls but am I too tall? Is that what he means?" "WHERE R U? WAITING IN LOBBY." "HURRY UP" "JustJosh is tall. Maybe I should steal him from you." "J/K!" "Srsly, I wouldn't." "Or would I?" "Nah, my heart belongs to the Right Max." "CANT FIND U. R U STILL MAD?"

You've read them so many times now that you've memorized them:

*Stop calling him JoshHarris! His name is Josh! Just Josh.*
*Related: Why does he call you Schmidt? So unsexy, Nerdball.*
*Unrelated: Max says that he likes tall girls but am I too tall?*
    *Is that what he means?*

*WHERE R U? WAITING IN LOBBY.*
*HURRY UP*
*JustJosh is tall. Maybe I should steal him from you.*
*J/K!*
*Srsly, I wouldn't.*
*Or would I?*
*Nah, my heart belongs to the Right Max.*
*CANT FIND U. R U STILL MAD?*

It's poetic. It's more of a poem than any poem you know.

"Poems don't have to rhyme," you say, out loud, before Kath can correct you from wherever she is now. You shut your phone off.

You wish you hadn't upgraded it right before the trip. You wish you had thousands of Kath texts to memorize. You would devote your life to it, like those monks who are counting grains of sand on a beach. You would recite them without looking, rubbing each individual word in your mind like it was a wishing stone that could reverse time and save her.

"Josh Harris is *not* your type," you tell your silent phone. "But neither is Max. He's terrible. He's not good enough for you. Smelly breath! Predictable future! And he's too short. You're not too tall. The problem is *him*."

You won't be able to sleep. There's no chance. Your body is achy and euphoric, sore in a way that isn't sore.

*Spent*, you think.

You look up through the skylights. The stars are up there, but now clouds are starting to thicken the darkness. You take off your glasses and it all blurs together into a gentle haze of graying light.

"I love you, too, Josh Harris," you say out loud. "But what happens next?"

Your head feels heavy and your breathing feels labored. *What next, what next, what next?* you whisper. Your voice is gravelly and loose, rolling down a mountainside. You smell the burning fuel.

What now?

What else is there?

You fall asleep that way, Orange Rabbit in the crook of your chin, the iPhone in your hand, open to Kath's texts. You start to dream. In the dream, Kath is a bat, flapping around in your room, wings beating against the boards. In the dream, you're laughing. Kath's tiny face, smiling, hovering. *"You know,"* she says. *"I was thinking—"*

# 18.

THIS LITTLE SHOPPING excursion is part of the Program.

The Program, with caps like that. The Program is the brain-child of Dr. McDreamy, whose name you still can't remember. The thing is that after you've been on a plane that has crashed, you do things like move to Wyoming to join a program run by a man who looks like a doctor on TV. That's life.

Sometimes it makes sense, at other times not so much.

But here you are.

In a capital-P Program.

Dr. McDreamy is very big on *intent*.

The *intent* of the Program is to make you normal again, to undo whatever it was that happened to you—not to your body, but to your brain—when the plane left its flight path and dove, nose-first, into a mountainside.

Can that really be undone?

Well, with *intent*. Yes. That's what he says, and he is the expert.

The *intent* of the Program is to fix you. The part that is on you is to continue to live life until it feels like life is not something you stole from the two hundred and sixteen people who died on the mountainside, or before the plane even fully crashed, or in the explosion afterward. Normal is sometimes easy (when you're with Josh Harris) and sometimes impossible (when you aren't).

Existing as just yourself feels like a lie.

Without Josh Harris touching you, you feel as though you don't exist.

You aren't scared, exactly. At least you don't think you are. It's just that without him, you feel too exposed. You compensate for that by wearing layers of clothes, even though it's still summer-warm. Today: dark jeans; knee-high, laced-up boots (Docs); a hoodie over a T-shirt over a tank top. A cowboy hat, a real one, the first and only thing you've bought since moving to Wyoming.

The hat is because your hair is freshly purple. Purple seemed like the right choice for a new school, not to mention the new person you are now that you are no longer a virgin. It seemed like it would say, "I'm upbeat, yet slightly dark. Optimistic, but skeptical! Quirky, but with depth!" Also, it just *shows up* a lot more than white and maybe you want to be seen. White is for ghosts. Purple vibrates with *life*.

Purple is pretty.

*"Purple is trying too hard, is what it is. Especially with those glasses, Schmidt. It's like you Googled 'manic pixie dream girl' and went for it. And you know how we feel about that."*

"I know how *you* feel about that," you retort. "But I'm not you."

You have been a person with blue hair *Before*. (Kath didn't like that either.) So you can be a person with purple hair now. You understand that sometimes colorful people blend in better than people with no color at all.

*"You look sort of like Barbie, if Barbie had had a manic episode and dyed her hair an unnatural and terrible purple only ever seen before on the tail of a plastic My Little Pony. Not that any purple hair is natural, but there are gradations, one through ten, normal through My Little Pony's tail color of choice."*

Now, in the quiet of the feedstore, you grin and touch your hair self-consciously then tuck it behind your ear. Even the texture feels different, more *slippery*. Like a doll's hair or a wig. Maybe later, you'll wash it with dish soap, try to get it to look like something closer to lavender than violet.

Well, the hat covers most of it.

Suddenly, you want to get out of there. You want to go home to your perfect bedroom, climb between the cotton-smooth sheets. Hold very still. When your hair was white, it was camouflaged against the pillow. You truly fully disappeared into the bed. Was that what you wanted?

You feel dizzy. Off balance.

*You just have to order the stupid horse food! Act normal, remember? INTENT. Get control of yourself! Keep it together!* you tell yourself.

It's not fear, not exactly. It's more just an overwhelming desire to *escape*.

*"Nike: Just do it,"* murmurs Kath, right in your ear, like she's somehow shrunk herself down and is sitting on your shoulder. You twist your head, trying to see.

Of *course*, she's not there.

Of course.

She can't be.

That would be crazy and you are not crazy, you are normal. *Intentionally* normal. And Kath is dead.

You touch a notice on the board and fix your gaze on it, like it's not the only thing between you and free-falling through time and space. *Anchor.* You chant the whole rhyme in your head, but that word sneaks out and fills the space around you. You cough to cover it up. To make a sound that isn't nuts.

All this talking to yourself is almost definitely not going to make you popular at school. You mentally pencil it in as the first major change you need to figure out how to make, stat, in order to pass as *normal*, to be okay.

You tap the board, hard enough to hurt your finger, like you're carefully considering something posted there. It is covered with ads offering riding lessons, horse boarding, housesitting, babysitting, and one used truck for sale. Your eye drifts around, not really seeing, trying to grab something to focus on. The truck, the truck, the truck. You try to make it come into focus. It's bright red. The photo is a Polaroid, shiny and out of focus. You blink. You see yourself in the truck.

You blink again, and you're gone.

You want the truck.

Of course: Your first car should be red; it should be a truck.

"I'm not sophisticated," you tell Kath. "That's your job. I'm a girl who drives a pickup truck. Bright red. I'm a girl who goes to country concerts. And I like it."

*"Country is music for people who have no imagination beyond feeling like Eeyore about heartbreak and their dead dog."*

"Yeah, well, maybe I *am* Eeyore," you whisper. Then you tear off the loose tab with an email address on it.

You are seventeen, after all.

It's time: to drive, to own a red truck, to have all the freedom that comes with your license. All the others died before they got this far. You'll do it for them.

Why not?

You scrunch the paper up into a tiny ball and jam it into the front pocket of your jeans where you'll have the option to forget about it.

Or the option to buy it.

"I'll go out more, I promise," you imagine telling your parents. "I'll drive myself places. Alone. You'll see. So *normal*."

Normal! The holy grail! Goal achieved!

They'll high-five each other or even hug (reconciled by your efforts!) and smile at you proudly and you'll drive to school like everyone else, your ticket to freedom parked in the lot beside the gym or wherever it is. It's not like you don't know how to drive. You don't grow up on a farm, even if it's a peach farm, without knowing at least that. You suddenly yearn for that truck with such a fierce longing that it catches you off guard. You *have* to have it. Maybe it's your inner country girl coming out. It was always in you, buried beneath your pony dreams and your search for the perfect colorful leather cowboy boots. Kath would laugh at you so hard. She's a sports car girl, to the bone. Her first car would be a Ferrari. A Maserati. Something with a gold logo involving a stallion.

You text the photo of the truck to her. "Too country?" you type.

Behind the counter, a boy around your age (who looks a *lot* like a young Benedict Cumberbatch) is chewing on a pen cap and staring like it's not rude. You pretend you can't feel his eyes burning a hole in the back of your skull. You keep studying the board like there's an answer to a question you didn't ask.

Everything is like this now: fuzzy, slow-motion, like a heart trying to beat when your veins are filled with mud.

Why? Why? Why?

And then, there, in the bottom corner of the bulletin board, like a light is shining on it: a flier no bigger than a Post-it note. SURVIVORS' GROUP: FOR EVERYTHING THERE IS A REASON. WHAT IS YOURS? Then an address, *1430 Old Main Road, back entrance.* And a time, *7:30 p.m.*

"Probably just Bible thumping," you say, out loud. "Touchers. That type." The boy clears his throat and then thumps on the counter, one, two, three times. You pretend not to notice.

The date on the notice is today's date.

*"Duh, it's a sign."*

You take a photo of the information with your iPhone for no reason. It's stupid. It's not like you'd ever go to a *Survivors' Group*. It sounds too much like something your parents would get excited about, or at the very least, something from a John Green novel, and this isn't that. This is your life.

On the other hand, Dr. McDreamy would be so proud. So much *intent*!

Before you can stop yourself, almost like your fingers have an *intent* of their own, you text the photo to Josh Harris. "B there or b □?" you type, then hit Send before you can change your mind.

The boy behind the desk thumps on the counter again, drumming to a song that is not the one playing through the speakers. You get it, he wants to get your attention. "Thump, thump, thump," like how on the plane on the way to France, the Right Max kept kicking the back of your seat. Each time, you swung around and glared. Every time, he said, "Sorrrrryyyyy," in a tone that meant he wasn't even a little sorry.

*Thump, thump.*

You don't really have any choice, you have to order and pay for the feed and arrange to have it delivered. You turn around. You face him.

You can do this.

You can be normal with *intent*.

# 19.

"WELL, HELLO, FINALLY," the feedstore boy says. "You're new. You're going to buy that truck. And you'll look good in it. I'm Dwayne." He has a sharply cornered English accent, so crisp that it makes you think of toast, neatly de-crusted with a sharp bread knife. A perfect square.

"Dwayne," you repeat. Then, "You're *English*?"

"Dwayne," he confirms. "I'm English. So, you're new then. Let me guess: College? High school? Tourist?"

"Do you get a lot of tourists in the feedstore? Buying souvenir chicken feed? God, you look exactly like Benedict Cumberbatch. I have to place an order for my horse. Food." You wave the piece of paper around with the information on it, like he might think you're lying, like you *might* actually be a tourist who wants to just idly observe how people live in backwoods Wyoming, stalking feedstores for entertainment, seeking saddle soap.

Benedict Cumberbatch is your celebrity boyfriend. Your top pick. He always has been. You obviously can't tell this *Dwayne* that, but you're desperate to take a photo, text it to Kath.

*"Now you have a quandary, you've got JOSH HARRIS ALL ONE WORD making oh-so-sweet love to you on a football field. And now Benedict Cumberbatch Junior eyeing you like you're a piece of steak on a grill and he hasn't eaten in months. What to do?"*

"Oh, shut up," you whisper, but you angle your phone, still, trying to get the pic discreetly.

"Aren't you lucky? We happen to sell *just* what you need," he says. "Let me see that." He plucks the paper out of your hand. "Gum?" He offers you an open pack, one stick half out already.

"I don't chew gum," you say. "Gum kills. A fifteen-year-old in Wales died in 2005 after chewing fourteen sticks of gum per day for, like, ages. I don't know how long. But still, dead is dead."

"Hmm," he says, withdrawing the pack. "Well, I suppose I wouldn't want you to die. Especially on this, your lucky day."

"Right, it's just like I won the lottery! To find that the feedstore sells . . . feed. What kind of English person names their kid Dwayne, anyway?"

"The kind of English person who is American," he says. "My father is American. My mum raised us in England but graciously allowed him to pay the bills and to choose my name.

My sister is Poppy, which is a proper London girl's name. But now we're here. In Wyoming. Or Why Oh Me, as I prefer to think of it." He makes a theatrical swooning gesture when he pronounces it out: Whyyyy ohhhh meee! "Dad runs the stable down there"—he points—"and owns this shop. He's kind of a big deal. You'll hear about him, if you have a horse. Rode for the Olympic team in the 1980s."

"Why Oh Me doesn't actually make sense. And Poppy is a pretty strange name for a human girl. It's a dog's name."

"Why Oh Ming doesn't exactly make sense either," he says. "And Poppy is a lovely name, don't be cheeky. Fits in well in London, which is really all that matters. I'm going back as soon as possible. America is *not* for me."

"Did you know that the number one cause of selfie-related deaths in America is when people pose with guns and the guns go off?" you say.

"You have a very peculiar *thing* about you," he says. "I like it. I'm not anti-selfie-death-by-gun, though. Most self-ies are a crime against humanity. Nobody needs to see that many duck lips."

"Do you miss the double-decker buses and the jumpers and things then?" you say, mimicking his accent. "Is that why you're going back?"

"Not bad," he says. "A little too Cockney. You could stand to sound more posh. Like me."

"I'll practice up in all my spare time," you say.

"Ahhhhhhh. Aren't you just an American manic pixie dream girl?" He smiles widely. "I thought your type only existed in films. This is quite exciting."

"We do," you say. "I'm not real."

"Mmmm-hmmm, you've got it, definitely. The whole thing with the hair and the glasses . . ." He gestures at your face. "Cowboy hat, although we are in Wyoming, so maybe that's par for the course. *And* the fact you're American can't be helped. But you still have it: You're sarcastic. Perky. And the knee-high Docs are totally on point. You're adorable."

You raise one brow, slowly. "Unlike most people you've met in Wyoming? They weren't American?" You blush. "Anyway, I'm not *perky*," you say. "I'm American but I'm not anyone's manic anything. I used to try to be but it turns out that I'm just me. What you see is what you get. And if you think about it, manic pixie dream girls in movies only exist to make the boys into better people. Those movies are always about the *boys*. The MPDGs are props." You start to feel annoyed when you realize how true that is. "I am nobody's prop. So tough luck."

"You're no one's prop," he repeats. "Yes. I can see that. But frankly, I'm already eight percent in love with you and we've only just met."

You give him your sourest look. "Well, too bad. I'm taken."

He holds up his hands. "Fine! I'll back off." He grins. "It's working already. Down to seven percent."

"Ha ha."

He starts to walk around the store, gathering things. "You'll want this, and this, and this." The pile on the floor grows. You don't know what most of it even is. Why did you think you could take care of a horse? You haven't got a clue.

"I'm sorry, Midi," you say in your head. "You deserve better."

"Better than what?" says Benedict Cumberbatch.

"Better than nothing," you say. "I didn't say anything."

"But you did. It sounded clever, like a line from a sitcom. Are you an actress?"

"No."

"Please say you're an artist?"

"I guess. But don't get excited."

"Stamford High?" he says.

"Yes. I mean, not yet. But starting next week. You know, when school goes back. I don't go extra early because I just can't wait or anything. Not to mention the fact that I'm sure there are no teachers there presently and the doors are locked."

"You're babbling. I make you nervous, right?" He grins. "That's because you think I'm charming. I'll see you around school, Pixie. And I'm keen to see how you'll make me a better person and so on. Quite exciting. Were you trying to take a photo of me? Because you just have to ask. I'm happy to pose." He holds his hands against his face, smiles coyly.

You glare at him. "I told you. I'm just a *person*. You'll have to make yourself a better person all on your own and from what I've seen, you've got your work cut out for you. And I'm not trying to take a photo! There's terrible reception in here. I'm trying to send a text, as it happens."

"Okay." When he smiles, a dimple on his left cheek pops in so far, you could store a cherry pit in there. "Hang on two secs. Don't go anywhere." He smiles wider. "Sounds like I said sex, doesn't it? You're blushing. SEX. There, I did it again."

"Pith you," you mutter, but he's ducked down behind the counter and luckily he doesn't hear you. You wouldn't be able to explain. Where did that come from, anyway? It's like your past leaks out of you sometimes, like you're a balloon with tiny pinholes in it and little puffs of your former self come out when you don't expect it. Dwayne/Benedict Cumberbatch is fiddling around with something that you can't see.

"Hurry up. I have to go," you say. "My dad is waiting in the car."

"Oh, sorry." His voice sounds muffled. Then suddenly he's up, but wearing a giant horse head. You scream, both shocked and laughing at the same time. "That's 142.99," he says, through the horse's nostrils, in a normal voice. "Are you paying with cash?"

"Credit," you say, acting normal. "That's creepy, FYI." Your phone buzzes. "And it scared me half to death. Are you always this weird?"

You glance at the phone: Josh Harris. You are confused for a second, like you're being pulled out of one life and into another. Then, in the same instant, you're flooded with relief.

Josh Harris isn't exhausting.

Josh Harris doesn't *banter*.

His text says: "What is this survivor group?" A string of puzzled looking emoji faces.

You type back. "Pick me up at 7?"

"OK yes. But still???"

"The boyfriend?" says Benedict Cumberbatch, through the horse's nose, running your mom's credit card. He cocks his horse head in your direction.

"Wrong again, Benny," you lie, smoothly. "My dad wondering if I'm ever coming out of this store. Take that off. You look ridiculous."

"Do you go everywhere with your dad? Is he basically your bodyguard then? Are you famous? I didn't ask. I should have asked. Of course you are. You have that look. That It factor. What's your name? I want to Google you. Is it rude to tell someone that you're going to Google them?"

"You ask a lot of questions for a feedstore clerk," you say. "Can't I just buy food for my horse?"

"I suppose," he says. "Less fun that way, though."

He takes off the horse head and then before you have time to react, he grabs your hat and swaps it out for the horse mask, which drops down over your head.

Inside the horse head, it smells like plastic.

Yellow plastic.

You start to gasp. You're panicking before you're even aware that the smell is the smell of the mask on the plane. You can't get your breath. Great. You crouch down, then slide down to the floor. Gasping, gasping. You can't breathe. In, out. Out, in. You're drenched in sweat, shivering. You're going to die, here on the floor of the feedstore. That's probably ironic but right now all you care about is that you're going to die.

*Umbrellas*, you think. *Conundrum.*

"Are you okay? God, I'm so sorry! I was just horsing around. See what I did there? *Horsing* around?" He has pulled the horse head off you, awkwardly. You stay there, curled up, like a collapsed runner at the finish line of a marathon, breathing raggedly, unable to straighten your body.

"Do you need some water? I'm seriously sorry." His head is bent over so close to yours that you can smell his breath.

You can see the freckles across his nose, a picked-at zit on his cheek that has scabbed over. You hold up your hand and whisper into his ear, "Fuck off, Benedict Cumberband."

He shakes his head, standing. But not before you're hit by a waft of cereal milk and cinnamon gum. "It's *Cumberbatch*. If you're going to call me by the wrong name, it may as well be the *right* wrong name." He sounds slightly less confident than before. He holds out his hand, like he wants to help you up, but you ignore it and he drops it down by his side, looking at it like he's not sure what it's doing, like it's operating without his authorization, a feeling you're awfully familiar with. "Sorry," he mutters again.

Your heart still feels wobbly and so you hate him, but your breathing is starting to slow. You can feel sweat trickling down the back of your neck. It's too hot. It's too hot for what you're wearing. It's too hot for plastic horse heads. "I hate you," you whisper. Then, louder, "Forget it. Forget all of it."

"You don't mean that," he pouts. "You find me charming."

You shake your head, staggering to your feet. "Whatever, *Ben*."

"I think I'll bring you that feed myself, " he says. You can tell he's trying to sound confident, but he's failing. "There's something really fascinating about you."

"Sounds stalker-y," you say, rallying. "Cumberbutt, I'm telling you, that might fly in London, but in America, we don't take kindly to that kind of crazy."

"See you at school, Pixie," he says. "I'll show you around."

"I think I'll manage," you say. "Long hallways, numbered classrooms, right? The gym is the big open space with painted lines on the floor? The cafeteria is the room with the food? Thanks, though."

"That's my truck, by the way!" he calls after you. "I'll make you a deal on it!"

You wave your hand in the air. "No, thank you! I'm really more of a car girl, I think."

You push the door open and the warm outside air hits you hard. It's even hotter outside than it was inside. You're dressed all wrong. Layers are useful but also stupid when it's 90 degrees. You need to get home, change into a T-shirt and jeans, saddle up Midnight for a ride up the hill to the stream, let him wade through the water, the icy coldness pouring over your legs.

The thing is, you don't remember learning to ride, but you must know how.

Do you?

You pause, confused. You know you ride him all the time. You know you do. You wouldn't get that wrong.

But when did you learn? Who taught you?

You swallow hard. There's a bad taste in your mouth: smoke and acid. It's best not to look too closely at the details sometimes, that's all. The details can trip you up.

You can see your dad, waiting in the car, pretending not to be watching you impatiently, because *Chopped* starts in twenty minutes and he hates missing it and refuses to figure out how to record things on the cable box.

You wave at him.

Every time you do something alone, your dad acts like you've just crossed the finish line in first place but he's always been like that, even *Before*. It's the completely true and totally cringeworthy story of your life. You can count on your dad being there with, say, a huge sign that says GO ELYSE GO at a debate meet, and a ridiculously gigantic bouquet of flowers at every band concert. If you'd ever won first place in anything, he'd probably have had a stroke and dropped dead on the spot, so luckily you've never been the first across any finish line.

Kath is the athletic one. Not you.

*Was.*

"What, Dad?" you say, sliding into the passenger seat. "You look like you're about to burst into applause, give a standing ovation."

Your dad turns down the stereo, which is blasting classical music. You shiver. *Flutes.* Bile rises in your mouth. "Seriously, Dad, turn that off."

He reaches out and taps the button. The sound of a pop song you've never heard floods through the car. You relax a little. "Great job!" he says. "How did that feel?"

"Dad." You roll your eyes. "I ordered food for Midi. It felt like a feedstore. It felt like I ordered food for a horse. It's no big whoop. I don't know why we couldn't take it now, though. Why does it have to be delivered? It's just food! We could probably jam it all in the back, somehow."

He shrugs. "New car smell!" he says. "Once we start using it for animal stuff, then it's got that . . ."

"Old animal food smell?"

"Exactly," he says. He starts the car and pulls slowly out of the parking lot, like he's avoiding the nonexistent pedestrians and rush of imaginary traffic. He signals and looks both ways before inching out onto the main road. Then, "I'm proud of you, kiddo. Baby steps."

"Come on, Dad. I didn't *do* anything! I just don't like crowds of people pawing at me in case touching me is magic, which isn't that weird when you think about it. Most human beings don't like to be touched. The feedstore had no pawing crowds. Like, literally no other customers. Anyway, can I go out tonight? Me and Josh Harris are going to go to a thing."

"A *thing*?" He coasts to a stop at a stop sign. The road is completely empty in all directions, but he remains stopped. The phrase "abundance of caution" jumps into your head.

"Dad, *drive*," you say. Next to the car, there is a tree that at first glance looks like it is covered with crows, but when you look closer, you realize that they are shoes. *Shoe tree,* you think.

You remember drawing one once. A project about Wyoming you did for school? "The shoe tree," you mumble. Your brain is reaching for something it can't grasp. You look back at the road. "Dad, there are NO OTHER CARS. Go already!"

He presses the gas and the car tentatively rolls forward. "What kind of thing? Will there be crowds?" He speeds up a little and you relax, the shoe tree behind you.

"Nothing." You roll your eyes. "There are no crowds in this town, period. It's not like at home. I mean, it is home now, but you know what I mean. Anyway, we're just going to hang out, you know?"

"Okay," he says, slowly. "But you wanted a horse, you have to exercise your horse, that's part of the deal."

"I'm going to ride when I get home! Don't worry about it! I already planned to! I was just asking about *later*."

He smiles. "You can go out *later*, of course. I'm just curious because you don't usually ask, you usually *tell*. So it makes me think there's something else you want to tell? About later?"

"Geez," I mutter. "Just trying to do the right thing here." Then, louder, "Nothing to tell, Dad. Sorry. School starts next week, it might help if we know more than just each other, you know?"

"I'm making duck confit tonight. Will you be home for dinner?"

"I guess."

"Fair enough then," he says. He starts to hum. It sounds a little like *The Prisoner's March*.

157

"Dad," you say.

"What's that?" he says.

You barely get the window open before you throw up. The puking sneaks up on you all the time. You have almost no time to react before it's happening.

"So much for that new car smell," he says, sadly.

"Sorry, Dad," you groan. "I don't know what happened. I guess I just . . . Maybe it was something I ate."

He shrugs, but he looks really annoyed. "Cars can be cleaned," he says. "Let's get you home and cleaned up. You may not want to go out with Josh tonight anyway. Wonder if you're coming down with something."

"Josh Harris," you say, "All one word." But he's not listening. Then, "I'm not sick. You know it sometimes just happens. It's not the flu, the plane *crashed*."

Your dad doesn't seem to hear you, or at least, he doesn't answer. He's turned the radio up again and his eyes are on the horizon, where the sun is shifting slightly lower in the sky. Soon it will disappear behind the mountains, which are all around your little town, leaving them to cast shadows over everything, making the evening light gray and cool.

# 20.

You FIND YOURSELF arriving at the barn, having ridden, without remembering *where* you rode. Your legs ache pleasantly. Midi is sweaty.

It's not shocking, not really.

Not anymore.

Still, there's a mild jolt of "uh-oh" when you look down and see that your jeans are soaked and Midnight's flanks are muddy and you've already been wherever you went. Evidence. You have evidence. You shake your head hard from side to side as though that could dislodge a better image of what happened, of where you were. But there isn't a single image stored, just the feedstore, the horse head, then now, muddy jeans, sweaty horse.

You feel in your pocket for your phone but your phone is not there. If it were there, maybe there would be photos.

Maybe.

If you had taken any.

Your dad is in an empty stall in the barn, sanding a piece of wood that is going to be a sign at the gate at the end of the driveway. "Schmidt's Creek" he's calling your new home, which he finds wildly funny, as a pun on both your name and a TV show that he watched while you were in recovery. "In Recovery" is sometimes something you think of as an actual place, a holding tank where you existed in another space and time, a sort of purgatory that you can't remember but also can't forget.

"Hey," you say.

"How was your ride?" he says, looking up, balancing the sanding block on his bent leg. "Getting cool up there?"

"Yep," you say. "Sure is. I have to go take a shower. How's that duck coming along?"

"I'll get Midnight settled for you," he says. "I'll make you a taco. Turns out the duck is still frozen. Can you believe that?" He shakes his head. "Your mother forgot to take it out of the freezer."

"Thanks, Dad. Sorry about your duck, I guess."

"You okay, kiddo?"

"Sure, why wouldn't I be?"

He gives you a funny look. "No reason."

"I'm fine. I wish you and Mom would stop acting like I'm going to break. I'm not! If I were breakable, I'd already be broken."

"I know! Go! Shower! Have fun doing whatever nothing that you're doing!"

"Thanks, Dad. I'm sorry. I don't know why . . ." You wish *these* little pieces were the ones that you forgot, the awkward way you don't fit into your present.

You give Midnight a nuzzle, nose to nose. "Hope we had fun," you whisper. Midi pulls back a little, rolls one eye at you. You take a big lungful of horsey air and hold it in, letting it out slowly. Your dad starts sanding again, the sandpaper scratching against the wood. You lead Midi to his stall and go through the motions of taking off his saddle, brushing off all the dirt and leaves and muck that have stuck to him. His flank quivers. "You okay, boy?" you say.

"I said I'd do it," your dad says, quietly, from the door.

"I like doing it," you say. "It's fine."

"Won't you be late?"

You shrug. "It's not a big thing, Dad. It's not important."

"Sounded like it might be, that's all."

You finish with the brush. "I'm just going to turn him out for now, okay?"

"Sure." He stands there, staring at you, like he's waiting for something.

"*Dad*," you say. "Just stop."

"Dads worry, it's what we do."

"Well, you shouldn't." You put the brush away and hang the saddle. "Later, Dad."

"I'll come up and get that taco going for you," he says.

"You know what? I'll eat after. I'm not hungry. I feel sort of sick from before."

"If you're sure," he says. "I'll get Midnight here taken care of and finish this sign."

"I'm sure."

"Well, if I don't see you tonight, have fun!"

"Everything doesn't have to be fun!" you say. "What is everyone's obsession with fun, anyway?"

"Better than not having fun, I guess," he says. His brow is wrinkled up in his worried way, which makes you feel inexplicably furious.

"Sure, I guess," you relent. "Anyway, I'll see you later."

"Midnight curfew," he says.

"Whatever, Dad." You roll your eyes. "Midnight."

"Twelve thirty, then," he amends.

You wave your hand and head up to the house, your feet sinking into the soft, muddy dirt. You try to think about what you should wear. What do survivors wear? Armor? Jeans? A dress? You can't remember why going to this thing seemed like a good idea, but it did.

It seemed *imperative*.

Forgetting things, feeling like your brain is a sieve, is the most frustrating thing you've ever experienced. Your brain sticks, and scratches, like a record on one of Kath's brothers' record players that they set up in their garage like a DJ studio. You wonder if they still have that, if—even with her gone— they still spin their records, if there is someone in there who is not Kath, dancing. You sit down on the front lawn and pick a few daisies, string them together in a chain. The act of sticking your thumbnail through the daisies' stems reminds you of Kath.

*Kath, Kath, Kath.*

Everything reminds you of Kath.

"Kath," you say. "What is happening to me?"

"*Well, figure it out. Duh. I'm a goddamn shooting star. Are you happy?*"

"Yes," you whisper.

"*Focus on that then. Never rush to the ending, that's my advice. And it's actually really good advice for a change. Stellar advice, you might say. You'll know how it ends soon enough.*"

"But why can't I remember? What am I *missing*?" You reach for a daisy with pink around the edges, like it's been dipped in paint. You add that one to the end and perch the whole thing on your head. "Am I going crazy?"

You wish more than anything that she'd just answer already, that she'd give you some kind of a sign.

You have to know.

You want to know.

Sort of.

But there's nothing more from Kath, just the wind bending the grass and the sound of your breathing, the steady thumping of your heart in your chest.

# 21.

AND NOW, AS abruptly as if you've turned a page and found that ten or so pages were missing, here you are.

Did you say goodbye to your mom? Did you shower? You clearly changed—you're wearing a floral dress that looks like something Sandra Bullock wore in *Hope Floats*, a non-80s, non-teen movie that, for whatever reason, Kath loved.

Your hair is faded so you must have washed and rinsed and washed and rinsed and washed and rinsed a hundred times. You're wearing cowboy boots that you don't recognize: soft, perfect leather. Pale blue stitching in a pattern.

You are sitting in the front seat of Josh Harris's Volkswagen Beetle. You know it's his but you don't remember seeing it before. It's a ridiculous car for him. He's too big for it or it's too small for him. He has to fold his body in order to fit into it, like human origami.

"Nice car. Did you ever think about getting one that fit?"

"Funny, Schmidt. But do you have to say it every time? I love this car. It was my mom's."

"I'm sorry, I guess I forgot." You feel queasy. "I'm so sorry. How could I forget something like that?"

He shrugs. Something is different about him. He seems tired. Maybe even a little tired of you. But that can't be. This is your perfect romance. You reach over and touch his arm and he puts his hand over your hand and suddenly you're breathing again, but you didn't know you'd been holding your breath. "Tell me again why we are doing this?" he says. "This Survivors' Group? You look really, really pretty, by the way. You look amazing."

"Thanks. Why are we going? I guess because we *survived*. Maybe we'll find our people there. That's what would happen in a movie. We'd be a band of misfit friends, brought together by tragedy! It's like a kind of sad party. This is our kind of party." You think about it for a minute. "Not the kind of party with so much noise, you know?"

"Won't the others mostly be old? I think of survivors as being old people, who lived through cancer or were maybe drug addicts."

You shrug. "I have no idea. I didn't even know Survivors' Groups existed."

"I've heard of them. I've never wanted to go. It's not the first time it's come up. When I was little, my dad went to one and he wanted me to go but I was just a kid. I didn't know what they were and I sure didn't want to find out. Maybe it will be fun? Anyway, totally worth it to go there with you in that dress. I've never seen you in a dress. When did you get it?"

"I have no idea, okay?"

"Are you mad?"

"NO! Yes! I don't know! Forget it. Let's just get this over with. You're probably right, it's a stupid idea."

"I didn't say it was a stupid idea. But you hate this kind of thing. We'll have to talk about the plane crash. When we tell our story, we're going to be the ones who are different. And they may have good reason to want to touch us. If there are touchers anywhere in Wyoming, they'll be in this group. Are you sure you want to?"

"I used to be really scared I'd get cancer," you say. You lean your head against the glass, which feels cool and solid against your skin. "I used to Google things all the time, like 'Early symptoms of leukemia.' 'Do I have lymphoma?' It seems so dumb now."

"We could just go somewhere and . . . you know," he says. "I brought beer and snacks, just in case."

"I can't explain it, okay? I just feel like we *have* to go to this dumb meeting."

"Okay, okay," he says. "You win. But if it's boring, it's not my fault. Is it going to be like AA?"

"Have you ever been to AA?" you ask. "You're not an alcoholic."

"No, but I've seen it in movies."

You roll your eyes. "Well, then, sure. It will be just like that. Styrofoam cups of coffee and Oreos. Do you think that

Oreo is the official cookie of AA? They always have them on TV."

"Do they? I imagine homemade oatmeal cookies with big chunks of grains because someone traded their love of alcohol for a passion for wheatgrass."

"I *definitely* don't think wheatgrass cookies are a thing at AA meetings."

"Well, they should be. If we come to a second meeting, I'm going to bake some."

"Since when do you bake? You don't bake!"

"You don't know everything about me, Schmidt. I happen to be a great baker."

"I'll believe it when I see it."

"I'll have to show you one day. I'll make you a cake. Red velvet."

"Mmmm, sounds good. But hard pass on the wheatgrass."

*"Nice rhyme, Elyse Fleece. You've still got it. But why are you going to this meeting? He's right, it seems dumb."*

"Just because it's not something you'd do, doesn't mean it's dumb."

"Hey!" Josh Harris holds up his hand. "Calm down."

"I *am* calm," you say, but your jaw feels clenched. You want one of those beers now. Something. Anything to make you feel looser, more okay in your skin. "Let's have a beer. If this were AA, we couldn't, but it's not, so we can." You run your fingers through your hair. It feels sticky with sweat or who knows what.

"Your hair looks pretty."

"Thanks," you say. It's nice that Josh Harris compliments you so much, but is it too much? Is it that he doesn't have anything else to say? You squash that feeling down. It's not like you're exactly the most scintillating conversationalist either.

You reach into the back and grab one of the bottles and twist it open, the cap sharp against your fingers. You think about how you pressed your finger against the hole in the glass on the airplane. *Why are you thinking about that now?* You tip the bottle to your lips and swallow, once, twice, three times, four, five, six, swallowing air that feels like a stone. The beer is too carbonated and burns your tongue and throat, then just for a second, you're choking, then you can breathe again.

You burp.

"Schmidt," says Josh Harris. "I can't tell you how gorgeous you look if you're belching like Fitzy after chugging a liter of Coke."

"Sorry. Surprise! I'm not perfect," you say. "Want one?"

"I'm driving," he reminds you, primly.

You roll your eyes. "Okay, Mr. Good," you say. "Be good."

"You're not very funny," he says, but he's laughing.

"Says you," you say. "There happen to be plenty of people who find me funny."

"Like who?" he says.

"Benedict—never mind," you say. "I mean, people. I don't know. I bet everyone here will think I'm hilarious."

"I'm not sure that even you could find something funny to say about a plane crash." He reaches over and plucks the daisy chain off your hair. You must have put it back on after showering. The flowers look limp and sad. He puts it on his own head. "I am the king," he says.

You snort-laugh. "I'm supposed to be the weird one in this relationship," you remind him. "Concentrate on being the normal one, okay?"

"I default to being the weird one, in the eyes of all white people."

"There will be other black people at school," you say. But suddenly you're not sure. Maybe there won't be. "Almost certainly. Besides which, standing out for being the only black dude in the room is different than standing out for wearing daisies in your hair. Give them back. They complete my look." You reach for them, but he's already putting them back. He rests his hand on your head for a minute, two.

"Which floor?" you hear Max say.

"I forget," mumbles Charlie Martin, who already seems drunk.

"Three," you say, glaring at Max, trying hard not to move in case Josh Harris's hand shifts from its current position.

"Almost certainly? Have you noticed how there are very few black people in this whole town?"

"Well, no. Not really. But I'll take your word for it."

"I'm the best one, the worst one, the weird one, the only one. Me. You don't know what it feels like because you're white."

"You are the best one. Okay? Even if there are a kajillion other people in the room, white, black, brown, whatever, you are always the best one. The best person." You chew on your lip. "Definitely the best looking."

He sighs.

"What? I get what you're saying. Kath was my best friend forever, remember? I might not be black, but I sure know what it's like to be, like, followed around a store by a detective who assumes you're shoplifting because he's a racist douchebag."

"Please don't do that."

"Do what?"

"That thing where you're like, 'Some of my best friends are black!'"

"Well, they are." You pause, gulp down the rest of the beer. "Were," you add, softly.

"I'm sorry," he says. "I mean, I'm not. The fact is that you're white and I'm not and it's just easier for you. But I feel like I shouldn't have attacked you. It's just strange living in a white, white, white town like this." He pulls the car over to the side of the road where the shoulder is a wide gravel swath. There is a view from here that is heart-stopping. It's easy to forget you live in the mountains until you come to the gaps and can see down into the valley. It looks like a green river. The gravel crunches under the tires. There's a cloud of dust. You cough. Josh Harris leans in to kiss you.

"We'll be late! Also, I have beer breath."

"Mmmm."

"Was that your version of a fight? It wasn't very fight-y."

170

"Yes, we did have a fight, Schmidt. And I won. The part where I won is the most important thing for you to take away from this conversation."

You shrug. "I don't mind losing to you," you say.

"I'm glad you feel that way, Schmidt."

*Elyse*, you think, but don't say. *Call me Elyse. If you call me Elyse, everything will be okay.*

Josh Harris pulls back onto the road again. You turn the radio on, but the music feels too sharp against your ears, crackling, so you turn it off again and close your eyes. The bottle of beer is cold and beading with condensation between your knees. When did you become a person who drinks beer?

Josh Harris signals and turns into a parking lot. He pulls the car into a parking spot between two trucks. Wyoming— this part of it, anyway—is definitely a truck kind of a place, everyone seems to have one. Everyone except Josh Harris. You feel tinier than usual in your tiny car between the two big trucks.

An image of a truck shivers into place in your memory, slowly coming into focus.

A red truck.

It is parked beside your barn.

It's your truck.

You know that's true and yet, when did that happen?

You are a person who owns a truck.

You are a girl who owns a red pickup truck and lives in Wyoming and wears cowboy boots and has a boyfriend named Josh Harris and a white horse named Midnight. You blink. It's like your own life keeps sneaking up on you and surprising you, jumping out from behind a curtain, shouting, "BOO!" and you don't know whether to be afraid or ecstatic.

"Nothing makes sense," you say, as though Josh Harris has asked a question. "Here goes nothing. We're here, right? Let's go in and see what this is all about. If it's terrible, we can leave. We can go make out somewhere. And have snacks."

"I sincerely hope it's terrible," he says. "This is a bad idea. I'm only going along with it because I like you." He's gripping the steering wheel, like he's nervous or something, but he can't be, because he's *Josh Harris*.

"Settle down there, cowboy," you say. "It's just one dumb hour out of our whole forever." You fling the door open hard enough that it dings the door of the truck next to you, which is rusty. Probably the person who owns it won't notice the new mark. At least, you hope not. And if they do, so what? What is a ding in a rusty door in the big picture? It doesn't matter. Not even a little. Not when you consider the things that do: *Life. Death. Choose.*

You step out into the parking lot. It's a stage and you are at the center of it. You turn in a circle, dress twirling around your legs, arms reaching up to the big Wyoming sky. Somehow you're able to see yourself from outside yourself. *It's like a film*, you think. *I look pretty.*

*"You look like you're showing off like whoa. When did you get all LOOK AT ME, LOOK AT ME? You aren't the Elyse who I know and love and who I am really mad at right now and forever. You're some different Elyse. Twinkle-Toes Elyse. If they sold you in a store, you'd come with a free-with-purchase unicorn. Who are you anyway?"*

172

You stop turning, dizzy, but then you start again because Kath is dead and you forgive her for that, for being dead, and you *are* pretty in your flowery dress and cowboy boots, spinning and spinning and spinning, the Earth turning you around and around even after you've stopped moving, a tilt-a-whirl of colors and smells. The air is green and dusty and smells like summer and leaves and gasoline and trees, and below all that, the hauntingly sweet smell of the wildflowers, which are everywhere everywhere everywhere.

You try to stay upright, dizzy like a kid, fighting your body's urge to just give in and fall. You are in charge here. You tell it what to do. *Stay, stay, stay,* you tell yourself. You don't exactly know what you mean by that, but no matter. You make an arc in the gravel with your toe, waiting for Josh Harris to unfold himself from the car and join you. He's standing by the car now. He's gulping down a beer in one huge swallow. You can see his Adam's apple bobbing up and down.

"Cheers," you call. "To *us*." You hold an imaginary bottle up and he tips his empty in your direction, pausing to put it into the back seat when he's done. A huge bird flies overhead, an eagle or a vulture, you're not sure which. The wind pushes the branches of the huge trees and the shadows move around you. It seems to take a long time for Josh Harris to join you, or maybe that's just time playing tricks on you again, stretching like taffy toward the horizon, where the sun is dipping quickly behind the mountains, dropping fast enough that, for a second, it looks like a fireball hurtling toward the ground.

# 22.

There was this one time, before Paris obviously, when you and Kath won a contest to go on an exchange program with a school in a town in Washington State. You took a train. The ride was the best part of the whole thing, the shimmy of the cars on the track, the way the outside passed by in a blur, the way the whole thing had the vibe of being in an old-fashioned movie: There were waiters with white cloth napkins draped over their arms, a dining car, sleeping bunks. All that was missing was old-timey music, the scuttling sound of a film reel unwinding.

The air in Washington was so sharp—it was a bad winter—that it felt like blades in your lungs. Every breath hurt. An ice storm coated everything in a layer of glassy coldness in a way that was both beautiful and scary. Every detail was *encapsulated*, frozen literally and metaphorically. Even the memories you have now of the experience are blurred slightly by half an inch of ice and magic.

You'd been expecting *snow*—the fluffy, snowman-building, snow-angel type—but it didn't snow at all, the whole time you were there. Instead, ice ice ice was everywhere. "Ice ice, baby." Kath was singing and skating on the sidewalk, making it look like a real rink and like she was an Olympian, twirling, her red coat spinning out around her legs. On the first night, you were woken in the middle of the night by the sound of a huge branch, weighted down by its icy coating, breaking thunderously off a tree in the backyard of the house where you were staying, and crashing mercilessly through the roof of the garage. The woman who owned the house had seven cats, who were constantly slinking around your legs, purring. Your first worry, when you heard the crash, was that they had all been killed. It wasn't rational, it was just the first thing that popped into your mind, half-asleep and startled.

You're allergic to cats.

When you arrived, the woman had said, "There were nine this morning but the vet put two of them down this afternoon." You hadn't known what to say to that, exactly, so you'd giggled, while Kath had hugged the woman and patted her back while she cried. Kath always knew what to do, while you hovered in the background like a gremlin, laughing inappropriately and cruelly.

The lady—you can't recall her name—showed you and Kath to your room, which was wallpapered in thick velvety floral prints, dusty cobwebs hanging in the corners of the ceiling. The beds were high and looked like beds out of a Victorian novel. There was a fireplace in the corner, and the air smelled like old, dead flowers. Cat hair covered everything. You took antihistamine after antihistamine and maybe you were slightly stoned by the medicine and that's why everything seemed both so funny and so surreal.

When the lady left the two of you alone, you and Kath climbed down the fire escape and wandered into town, where you ate at a restaurant named Piggy and pretended to be from another world. "Mars," Kath said.

"Not actually habitable," you said. "I read it in a book. But Jupiter—"

You'd both gotten the giggles so bad that you nearly peed your pants, although in hindsight, what was so funny? Why not Jupiter? You know that in Wyoming there was a landing strip, specifically built for natives of Jupiter to land on when they arrived. The Greater Green River Intergalactic Spaceport. "You laugh, but I'm going to move there one day," you'd said.

"To Jupiter?" She'd barely been able to get the words out.

"No! Duh, Wyoming. How can you not love a place that is so welcoming to Jupiterians?"

"I don't think that's a word," she'd said. "I worry about you, kid. But, if anything, they are Jupes, you Jupe."

"You're the Jupe," you'd said, and stuck out your tongue.

"I'd die before moving to Wyoming," she'd said. "Why Oh Me."

"That doesn't even make sense," you'd said.

Something passes through you that feels like an electric current, snaking from your brain and down your spine. *Why Oh Me.* Two memories layer over each other like ice on the leaves outside.

*I am the leaf*, you think, inanely.

Ice forms on your skin. It's so cold. You're shivering. But you shouldn't be cold. You're in the parking lot of the survivors' meeting in Wyoming. Somewhere on the other side of the mountains in front of you is the Greater Green River Intergalactic Spaceport.

You're so dizzy.

You shouldn't have spun.

Not so much.

Not like that.

Not like *rolling.*

You touch the folds of your cotton dress. *Touch,* you think. *Touch touch touch touch touch touch,* and you must look crazy, grabbing at your own dress like that, but you can't stop. The fabric is too soft to feel like anything, it's not enough, so you reach down and then you have a handful of gravel and you press it hard into your palms until it hurts and you can be okay again. You close your eyes, you concentrate on Washington, on Kath, on the memories frozen into your mind.

Everyone in Washington was wearing Gore-Tex and looked like they would only use mascara or highlighter or even lip gloss if threatened at gunpoint. You and Kath looked really overdressed. "For this, I did my hair?" she'd snorted. She'd had her hair braided before you left Cali, a billion teeny tiny braids snaking over her skull and held in place with shiny turquoise beads.

She looked amazing.

Always.

Of course she did.

She was wearing a floral dress. Much like the one you have on now, come to think of it.

*Exactly* the one you have on now.

But that's impossible.

The fabric gets blurry in front of your eyes. You scratch one sharp piece of gravel into your palm until it draws blood. Why is Josh Harris taking so long? You can't see what he's doing. Your eyes are blurred, you must be crying, but you have to stop crying. Being sad is a choice. Everything is a choice.

*Choose.*

"Hurry up!" you try to say, but your voice, like you, is trapped in ice. Most things, you can't remember. Now you are having a memory that you can't escape.

*Help*, you try to say. *Something is happening.*

*"I think you're glamorizing that memory there, Schmidty. It was so cold it hurt. All we wanted to do was go home. Like, it was actually painful to be there. It wasn't all good times and giggles, although my hair* did *look magnificent."*

The sidewalks were so slippery, you'd practically had to skate back to the house after stuffing yourself on chicken fingers and onion rings and French fries and potato skins, ordering more each time you finished a plate. It seemed somehow like calories didn't count while you were away from home, like your jeans wouldn't be made tighter by the gigantic ice cream cake you shared for dessert.

When you finally found the house where you were staying—you'd gotten surprisingly lost in the tiny town, mistaking south for north in the dark—your host opened the door grimly, furious. She thought you'd been kidnapped. She thought you'd run away and that she'd be sent to jail. "How dare you," she'd said, tears glittering in her eyes.

For the rest of the trip, you avoided her as much as possible. She put out food for you in the morning—stale pastries, old muffins—and each morning, you and Kath stuffed the food deep into the bottom of your backpacks. The school you were visiting didn't seem to know what to do with you, exactly. You weren't there for a reason, not with a club, it was just a random trade of you two for two of their students, who you must have passed on another track, your trains sliding past each other somewhere in Oregon. You were almost jealous of those students, who—under bright California skies—would be sitting in your desks in homeroom, going outside to eat lunch in the shade of the palm trees that the graduating class of 1987 had planted in the quad.

The Washington school was gray concrete and made you think of prison or skating rinks. The teacher who had arranged the trip was out with Norovirus and everyone else just seemed vaguely suspicious of you. The principal clapped his hands together jauntily and suggested that you simply observe. All the other students looked nervously at you with your then-pink hair and at tall glamorous Kath with her braids, so you were reduced to wandering aimlessly from classroom to classroom, pretending to *observe*, listening in on boring lessons that seemed to have nothing to do with you.

After a day of that, you gave up. You spent the rest of the week hanging out in the cafeteria eating huge chocolate cookies from a vending machine while everyone was in class, drawing comics while Kath instructed you on what to draw, and every once in a while muttering "How *dare* you" to each other and dissolving into giggles.

"What if," she said, "you could draw something into existence?"

"Like fame and fortune?"

"Yeah," she said. "Draw me on a stage. Draw me singing something."

"But you can't sing!"

"I can in a drawing, duh. Come on. Draw me in sparkles with fans screaming. Draw my future. Make me look super glam and rich and *famous*. Like Queen Bey herself."

You did it, giggling the whole time. You drew her on the cover of *People* magazine, complete with the masthead. Then you drew the Right Max next to her, looking slightly cross-eyed. You drew his tongue like a lizard's tongue, snaking out of his mouth and into her ear. "Gross!" she said, but she smiled a little, too. She hadn't admitted yet, not back then, that she *liked* Max, but you always knew. You could just tell.

You knew her so well.

You knew her better than you knew yourself.

"Now you," she said. "Draw your future."

You drew yourself and Josh Harris, not on a magazine cover, but in a simple room with cinder-block walls. Sitting next to each other on plastic chairs. You drew him holding your hand.

Kath had laughed and laughed and laughed, bent double like she did when she wanted to emphasize just how funny something was. "That's IT? You could draw anything! That looks like a scene out of a John Green novel. What is it, like a grief group? Church basement? Are you guys surviving cancer or something? You should draw him with, like, one leg. You could be . . . I don't know, in outer space! On a pile of money! Hanging with Bey and Jay! And you draw . . . AA?"

You'd laughed, too, partly because of the accidental rhyme and partly because you knew your fantasies were so mundane, but you didn't think it was *that* funny. Or maybe it was. But it was all you wanted. You and Josh Harris, sitting.

Holding hands.

You filled in some background in the picture to make it look less church-basement-y. You drew art on the walls. A picture window. A painting of a unicorn. Then, to make her laugh, you drew a huge pile of donuts. There had been donuts on the counter of the house this morning, yet laid out for you on the table were the same hardening muffins you'd been served all week. Kath had wanted to sneak a donut, but you'd stopped her.

"Mmmmmm, donuts," you said, between giggles. "Fresh, delicious donuts! The *donut* lottery! We won! We won!" You kept going, drawing more and more and more donuts; donuts spilling off the table, a sea of donuts under your feet and Josh Harris's.

Then you drew a cat.

"An escapee," you told Kath. "He didn't want to get taken to the vet. He knows it's a one-way ticket."

That day is the funniest day you can remember ever having, just you and Kath in the empty cafeteria in a school in Washington, tears streaming down your face, the whole memory now encapsulated like all the trees and leaves and grass, under a layer of ice, freezing it in time forever.

# 23.

You are sitting next to Josh Harris in a church basement on a plastic chair, holding his hand. Behind you, a table is covered with what can only be described as a donut buffet. Chocolate covered, glazed, jelly-filled, apple fritters, maple and bacon, sprinkles. On the wall, there is a painting of a unicorn, raising its hooves toward a rainbow. A picture window frames the view of the parking lot: a series of trucks and Josh Harris's VW lined up like a row of soldiers.

Your heart is beating almost out of your chest.

You don't know what to do or how to explain what is happening, which can't be real, but is, so you bite your lip so hard that you taste blood, the pain distracting you enough that you don't jump out of the chair to run out of the room, tearing at your dress—*Kath's* dress—while you scream. If it were a dream, it wouldn't hurt. You pinch the skin on your arm so hard so hard so hard that you can see the bruise forming. Your eyes sting.

*"That dress looks good on you, I don't know what you're freaking out about. If I looked that good in it, I'd wear it every day. But fashion isn't something that matters too much to me anymore, if you know what I mean."*

You press your fingers into your ears, like that could block out the sound of her, but it can't because it's not her, it's just the part of you that will always hold Kath. Your heart or your brain or both.

"Just like AA," Josh Harris interrupts your racing thoughts. "It's *always* a church basement. I feel guilty drinking that beer before. I don't think God approves of boys who drink beer."

"Yep," you say. Your voice is creaky, as though you've been asleep. It feels like an effort to talk, like the air in here is too thin. You hold more tightly to Josh Harris's hand. You're trying to remember what you were wearing in the picture you drew. Was it this dress?

Where did you get Kath's dress?

You have to remember, but it's impossible, impossible, impossible.

You peek down the top of the boots and see patterned socks. You know without knowing how you know that the socks are the kind with separate toes knitted into them. You don't remember putting them on. You've worn them before, you remember.

*"Plane socks. Everyone knows that your feet swell up on planes so you have to take off your shoes if you don't want to suffer. Always*

*wear plane socks. Look, I bought these for you." Kath was laughing.*
*The socks were striped and in between each stripe, unicorns galloped.*
*The colors were too bright, too silvery, too tacky and you loved them*
*and then she pulled up her jeans and showed you her own, matching*
*socks, toe socks, the worst best socks in the world.*

"I'm trying to think," you say, out loud.

"Sometimes it's better not to think," he says. "Unless you're thinking about me, then it's all good."

You stare at him. His skin is so smooth, it makes you want to cry. Doesn't Josh Harris ever get a pimple? Does he ever look anything less than perfect?

In your comic, he was wearing jeans and a white T-shirt and that's what he's wearing now but that doesn't mean anything because that's what he always wears. You wish your heart would calm down or your brain would shut up or both.

"Something is wrong," you try to whisper, but you can't. There is the squeaky sound of chairs being moved around, the clip-clopping of someone's heels on the floor. You can't look. The smell of the donuts is filling up your mouth and maybe you can't breathe and maybe *something is wrong.* You try to remember. You're trying to remember.

Then an image comes to you. Your comic. In the picture you drew, he was wearing a hat. A baseball cap, tipped sideways, like it had been shoved onto his head awkwardly. He was smiling. You exhale. He's not wearing a cap right now. It's okay.

You didn't *draw* this scene into existence.

You didn't make this happen.

It's a coincidence.

That's all.

The sketchpad burned when the plane crashed. It must have. You shoved it into the seat pocket in front of you. You imagine the way the plasticized safety instructions must have melted in the intense heat, the way the paper would have begun to burn and curl up, like leaves on maple trees when they start to turn, but faster and faster, blackening and then turning to dust.

You twist your head around, as though you're stretching out a kink in your neck. Your vertigo is getting really bad, the room determined to knock you sideways.

"Josh Harris, I love you."

"What? I can't hear you."

You shake your head. "Nothing."

*Something is wrong here*, you think.

That something is as real as the scraping sound of furniture being shifted on a dusty concrete floor. It's as real as the smell of donuts and coffee, emanating from the table in the back, which is piled high with so many donuts, as though they were expecting a huge crowd. It's as real as the warm air being pushed around by an antique-looking fan, which makes a tiny squeak at regular intervals as the face of the fan slowly jerks from left to right, spreading the heat, blowing a smell which is a combination of rust and dust into your hair, into your mouth.

You make yourself look up and look around. With *intent*. Dr. McDreamy would approve.

*"It's about reprogramming your brain to remember how to remember,"* he's saying, soothingly. *"You can do it. You can choose."* He

*stares into your eyes and for a second, you find yourself thinking,* God, he's really cute, *even though you know that's not appropriate and then he says in a voice that's not quite his,* "CHOOSE." *It startles you and you stand up, abruptly.* "That's all for today," *he says, in his regular voice.* "Keep up the good work." *You walk out of his office and into a hallway in a hospital. Someone is pushed by on a stretcher. A beautiful female doctor who looks suspiciously like Dr. Grey is leaning over shouting,* "Don't leave us, Mr. McMillan. Stay with us." *You can't find your mom or your dad. Where are they? Why did they leave you here alone? And then you're walking down the hall, which seems to get longer and longer with each step, and, finally, pushing open an exit door and there, parked in the lot, your red truck, the keys suddenly in your hand, like you'd been holding them the whole time. You get home without thinking about which way to go, as though your brain knows more than you do if you just trust it and let go. You let go.*

*You get home with* intent.

"What are you thinking about?" Josh Harris whispers.

You shrug. "I'm in the moment," you tell him. "I'm living with intent."

"I was right about being the youngest," he says. "I knew this would happen."

More and more people are shuffling in now, *shuffle* being the operative word.

And he was right: You and Josh Harris are the youngest people in the room by easily sixty years, except for the one thirty-something-looking guy, who is in a wheelchair, his pant legs hanging empty to the pedals where he has no feet to rest. Apart from the fact he's missing his legs, he looks a lot like most of the adult men you've seen around in Wyoming:

balding, bearded, burly. The three Bs. The other youngish person is obviously the group leader, a woman who looks a little bit familiar. She's jaw-droppingly gorgeous, everything about her seeming out of place here in this room. She looks like a movie star. She's even wearing a sweater that looks like spun gold, clinging to her in all the right places, unbuttoned to reveal enough skin that even you look twice. She's pulled her hair back into a ponytail and she is wearing brown tortoiseshell glasses, which keep slipping down her nose, but other than that, she looks almost red carpet ready.

"She's so pretty," you whisper to Josh Harris. "Oh my god."

He shrugs. "Not as pretty as you, Schmidt," he stage-whispers so loudly that the elderly woman next to you gives you a small smile. Her hair is tinted lavender, not unlike your own.

"He's sweet on you, honey," she murmurs. One dark hair pokes out from a mole on her cheek, like a spike on a cactus.

"I know he is," you say, hoping it doesn't sound as rude and abrupt as it feels. "He's my boyfriend."

"Oh, is he?" she says. "Well, that's nice. He's very tall."

"He is." You nod. "He's nice, too. I'm not just with him because he can, like, reach high shelves or whatever."

"Well, good," she says. "Nice goes a lot further than tall in the big picture."

"Yep," you agree.

You hear running footsteps in the hall, and then another girl, your age, bursts in.

"God, I'm so sorry," she says, in an English accent. She looks *so* familiar. "I'm Poppy. Hello there, everyone. Look at all of us, surviving! Go, us! Do I do a little speech or something? Everyone here is very old, aren't they? Maybe this isn't a good place for me." She touches her hair, tosses it like a horse flinging its mane.

You don't like her.

*"She's insufferable. Real shame that one survived. But then again, only the good die young. Not that* you're *not good, Schmidt.* You *are good. You're just a pain in the ass sometimes, you know?"*

"Survived what?" you say out loud.

"Gosh, weren't you listening? We've just been *told* we aren't at that part yet. Did you get a head injury when you survived your thing, then?" The British girl is talking directly to you.

You glare at her. "Yes, actually I did." *Traumatic brain insult,* Dr. McDreamy had said. *It may or may not affect your brain permanently.*

"Explains a lot," she retorts.

You wonder what would happen if you casually stood up and punched her right in her face. Your fist clenches. "Shhhh," says Josh Harris, like he's read your mind. "Don't let her bother you. She's on your side."

"I don't think being a survivor is actually a group effort," you say.

The leader clears her throat and stands up. "Well, then, let's get started."

Poppy pulls out a chair and sits down, noisily. Dramatically.

"Feedstore Dwayne!" you say. "You're his sister."

"Which makes you the Manic Pixie Dream Girl," she says, slowly. "Purple hair. I see it now. I would have pictured you . . . differently."

"Rude," you say.

"Hey," says Josh Harris, ineffectively.

The leader waits, watching you. When you don't say anything more, she continues. "I am a PhD candidate studying the effects of surviving something that no one expected you to survive. This can be an accident or a diagnosis. From a psychological standpoint, both are equally interesting."

"I guess we're not the only young people, after all," says Josh Harris into your ear. His voice gives you goose bumps, like it always does. "Who is Feedstore Dwayne?"

"No one," you lie, shrugging. "Nothing. I mean, I met him when I bought horse food. I guess she's his sister."

"She's pretty," says Josh Harris, like he can't help himself, like he's so overflowing with compliments, he's willing to even give them out to undeserving girls, like *Poppy*.

*"You sound like a bitch. Just because another pretty girl under the age of twenty is in the room doesn't mean that Josh Harris is going to fall in love with her. It must be exhausting to be so insecure. Snap out of it, Schmidt."*

You pretend to be tucking your hair behind your ears, but instead stick your fingers in them. "Shut up," you tell Kath. "Just stop. Please."

"Sorry," says Josh Harris.

"Not you," you say, but it doesn't matter.

You stay that way for one minute, then two. The leader is still talking, no doubt about the subtle difference between thinking you're going to die in a month from a brain tumor and believing you're going to die in two minutes on impact.

*Interesting, interesting, interesting. NOT.*

You are having a hard time tracking what she's saying. It seems like it has nothing to do with you and everything to do with you. Your mind skip-hops around in time. Kath is wearing the dress, swishing it around her legs. "You like?" she's saying. "I'm buying it." Midnight is whinnying in his paddock, nuzzling his nose into your palm and then suddenly throwing back his head. He looks like he's laughing. Josh Harris's face is above you, stars behind him, and he's going to kiss you, he is. And you—

Josh Harris nudges you. "Hey," he says, again.

It's your turn to speak.

All the eyes in the room are on you. Then Poppy says, "Oh, *I* know who you are, you're the plane crash survivors from California. Aren't you just darling in real life?"

So instead of talking, instead of saying the speech that you'd practiced in your head, you stand up and run out of the room, your cowboy boots clattering like hooves on the church basement floor, the fan blowing Kath's dress around your legs like a current in water, tangling you in yourself, threatening to trip you up.

# 24.

IT'S THE FIRST day of school and you're standing in front of a locker that you know the combination to, because it's your old combination from your school in California: 0–45–28.

You had to act unsurprised when the secretary handed you the piece of paper. You couldn't possibly explain it, so instead of saying anything, you laughed inappropriately. As you walked away, you could see her checking her teeth in the mirror, as though you were maybe ugly-laughing at some unforgivable hunk of spinach stuck in her teeth, as if you were that kind of person, who would laugh in someone's face.

Anyway, it's just a coincidence, the number being the same, like picking the right six numbers on a lottery ticket and suddenly finding yourself with millions of dollars. It happens. But there's no money involved, here, just a bright orange locker, empty. You half expected you'd open it and see all your old stuff: the shelf where you kept your hairbrush and a mascara and a lip gloss, the mirror glued to the door, the special jars that stuck with magnets, holding your favorite pens and hair bands. It's all so familiar at the same time as being new, the clanging of doors opening, the banging as they shut. You hang your backpack on one hook, your jacket on another. It looks so desolate, empty. Next to you Josh Harris is putting his backpack into his own locker. You get a whiff of him, toasty and soapy and perfect.

He looks over at you and winks. "We've got this, Schmidt. How hard can it be?" His head is freshly shaved and it makes him look younger, somehow, less Josh Harris–level sure of himself. He also looks beautiful.

And perfect.

And you are *so* lucky, that's what all the other girls here are thinking.

You know it.

You reach out and rub your fingers along his shaved skull, above his ear, glittering with the diamond he always wears. You—Elyse Schmidt—get to do that, because *Josh Harris is your boyfriend*.

He smiles at you. Your blood rushes to all the places that he's ever touched, all at once—*the field the field the field*—and you want to drag him by the hand out of the school, find a place where you can spread a blanket, press your naked self against him. It's been so long that maybe it didn't happen at all, or maybe it happens every day and it's just lost in the broken pathway in your insulted mind.

"I know," you say, instead. "It's going to be good. I mean, look at it. It looks like a high school in a book or something. It's so *clean*. Creepily clean, actually."

"I don't think cleanliness is creepy," he says, looking around. "It's very shiny. It just looks new."

"I like it, too. So far, anyway."

You don't mention the thing about the locker combination. If his is also the same as his old one that would no longer be coincidence. It would be something else. It would be something you have to figure out, forcing your brain to process it and disseminate it and decipher it until it makes sense. It's terrifying to consider, so you kiss him instead. Hard. *Velvety lips.* You kiss him even harder, until your teeth clatter together painfully.

His mouth always tastes exactly the same.

A passing teacher clears his throat, "Hey," he says. "No PDA in the halls, you know the rules."

"Sorry, sir," says Josh Harris, pulling away from you, rubbing his lip with his finger and looking at it as if he's expecting blood or some other kind of stain. "We're new."

The teacher is young, bearded, white, in a polo shirt with the collar turned up like the trying-to-be-trendy teacher in *Ferris Bueller's Day Off*. "Ah," he says. "The plane crash kids." He cocks his head to one side. "I'm Coach Sims."

"Please don't ever call us that," you say, shocked that he did.

That he would.

That it happened so fast.

"I'm sorry," he says, but you can tell that he isn't. "Call me Coach," he adds. "Everyone does. I have that *People* magazine in my office, you two on the front. Maybe you can come by and sign it."

"There is literally *no* possibility of that," you say, at the same time as Josh Harris is saying, "I don't think that would be very appropriate."

"Heh," says Coach Sims. "What a world." He sticks out his hand, as though he expects you to shake it.

"I don't touch people," you say, your smile stuck in place. "It's in my file. No touching."

"Oh, I wasn't *touching*, I was just . . ." He shakes his hand out like it's wet or as though he knows about the touchers, like he's found the website and seen what people have said about you and Josh Harris and the power they want you to have. You wonder what's wrong with him that he wants to fix, while pretending to not want it. You study his face. He has that look that some men have of wanting to be better looking than they are. Maybe he has an STD. You giggle. "Welcome to Stamford," he continues. "You're our first celebrities. It's a small school, only two hundred. You'll find your people. Make friends. All that. Hope you'll consider playing basketball," he adds to Josh Harris. "You played at your old school, right? We have a solid team."

"I'll think about it," says Josh Harris. "I haven't decided yet."

"I don't do sports," you say, to save him the awkwardness of asking you, even though he is already turning away.

As soon as he's gone, Josh Harris kisses you again, the kind of kiss you can feel all the way down to your feet, which are up on tiptoes so you can reach him and he can reach you. A gentle kiss, no chance of drawing blood.

The bell rings and only then does he pull away. People are staring, but you don't care.

Maybe you even like it.

You won't be invisible at this school, not like your last school, where it didn't matter what you wore or what color you tipped your hair, you were always in Kath's shadow.

Here, you are just you.

Here, you are Josh Harris's girlfriend.

A girl with teal and pink hair smiles at you, then walks away into a beam of sunlight shining in through the high windows. You're temporarily blinded, and when you blink, she has disappeared into the crowd.

"Hi!" you say.

"Who are you talking to?" asks Josh Harris.

You shrug. "I don't know."

"I'm relieved," he says. "I thought maybe you'd seen that girl, Poppy. The one with the secret survival story. She's the only other person you know here, right?"

"What was her story?" You're dizzy again, just like that. "I've forgotten."

"You stormed out. You were mad, remember? She said she couldn't tell anyone what happened to her because of her circumstances. Maybe she's on the run from the mob. In the Witness Protection Program."

"Yeah, she wishes," you mumble. "Too bad they didn't catch up."

"That doesn't sound like something you would say."

"Well, I said it, so I guess it is. I've told you before. I'm not a good person." You slam your locker harder than necessary and the sound feels like it rattles your bones, your spine, your whole body.

That day in the lake keeps surfacing in your memory: You, floating on the air mattress with Kath while her brothers swam around underneath, pretending to be sharks. You knew they weren't sharks—*obviously* they weren't sharks—but the possibility of them rising to the surface under the raft, upending it, dumping you into the cold water, gave you the creeps. Your mattress kept wobbling on the waves and you kept screaming and Kath kept laughing.

Why are you thinking about that now? It doesn't make sense.

*"We hold on to two types of memories the hardest,"* says Dr. McDreamy. *"The good ones and the bad ones. It's the ones that aren't extreme that we lose the most easily."*

The trouble is that so much of your life has not been extreme.

You clear your throat. It's not a frog, not exactly, more like something dry is stuck in there, scratching. In your comic about weird ways people have died, you drew a man who died the day after a cockroach-eating competition, apparently asphyxiating on cockroach legs that were lodged in his throat. "It's a metaphor," you wrote underneath it, but now you don't remember what you meant. Sometimes it feels like all your thoughts are slowly disconnecting from your other thoughts, pulling apart, leaving behind a void that's a blur of white noise and light, and you are falling into it and your throat is so scratchy and you need a drink of something, anything, and you cough and cough.

You gasp when Josh Harris puts his hand on your arm. He squeezes, maybe a little too hard. "Do you need the Heimlich maneuver?" He slaps you on the back hard, too hard, and it hurts, but the cough stops, at least.

"Are you okay?"

"Yes, stop hitting me," you say, trying to sound normal. Something is wrong, but you can't tell what it is, like when you are dreaming and the dream tips over into a nightmare and you're stuck on the border between the two, trying to awaken.

The school is so small, it feels like a soundstage more than a real place. It is so much smaller than your school in California. It is also picture-perfect. It is brick on the outside, with wide stairs leading up to the front door. The building itself has a series of angles that, from the outside, make it appear like the architect was maybe crazy, but on the inside, the angles translate to skylights and so much light every-where, spilling from the windows, filling the halls, cover-ing the walls with light so bright it's almost blinding. It's a movie-set school; it can't be real life. Everyone is too well dressed and looks too happy. No one is skulking alone by the lockers, trying not to be seen, like the Other Max back home, always waiting for some idiot to try to beat him up, or to stuff his head into his tuba.

You look back, over your shoulder, half expecting to see Charlie Martin, looking depressed about Kath still, his saxophone case strapped to his back. You need desperately to see Kath, bopping along down the hallway, listening to something, talking to someone, and gesturing with her hands all at once. If she saw you, she'd stop in her tracks. "You know, I was thinking—" she'd say, only this time she'd finish the sentence and you'd *finally* know what she was thinking, after all this time.

You search for her, suddenly believing that she might be here, after all. It's surreal, so why not?

But there is no Kath.

There is no Charlie.

There is no Max.

Instead, there's a sea of familiar-looking strangers who all look like people from TV shows you watched a long time ago. And Josh Harris had nothing to worry about, there are plenty of black kids.

Someone taps you on the shoulder and you jump, startled, too much adrenalin. You turn around, "Well, hello there, Pixie," says Benedict Cumberbatch, English as ever. "I was hoping I'd run into you." He glances at Josh Harris.

"And your rather intimidatingly good-looking boyfriend. I've heard all about *him* from Poppy. Speaking of, there she is! Poppy, it's the plane crash kids!"

"*Dwayne*," you say, twisting his name around in your mouth like metal. "Please don't ever—"

But next thing you know, Josh Harris—Josh Harris who has never been violent in his life—has Dwayne up against the locker, by the neck, feet dangling comically. He doesn't look like Benedict Cumberbatch up there: smooth, debonair, witty. He looks like a scared, scrawny kid with bad skin and an awkward accent. You almost feel sorry for him.

*Almost.*

"Part of the deal with Survivors' Group," you hear Josh Harris say in a voice you've never heard from him before, "which your sister would know if she'd bothered to listen, is that *nothing* leaves that room. Get it? Got it?"

"Yes. I get. I got. Could you please put me down? I'm afraid of heights. Nothing higher than a horse, that's my rule." His voice gives away his fear, or maybe he's just not that good an actor, after all.

"*I really don't get what so many people see in that guy. He's so wormy. Like he looks like a person who has actual worms. That degree of whiteness is just unhealthy and who is attracted to bad health? How is he so famously sexy? It's offensive to my eyeballs, actually.*"

Josh Harris lets go and Dwayne crumples to the floor. You're torn for a second. Do you help him up? Do you walk away? Your eye meets his and you shrug.

He looks away.

Your knees feel shaky and strange. You *remember* going to Survivors' Group with Josh Harris. You remember running out partway through. You remember him leading you back into the room, twirling you in the hallway outside first—once, twice—like you were about to step through time into a ballroom dance, your floral dress spinning around your legs. You remember Poppy appearing in the doorway and saying something sarcastic—what was it? Something like, "You people just never stop dancing, do you?"

You went back into the room and listened to Bo, the man with no legs, talking about how the tank he was in hit an explosive and was torn apart, his buddies dead in front of him, his own legs no longer where they should have been. "I thought I'd come back a hero," he said. "But instead, people react to me like I'm contagious, like if they actually got close to me, maybe they'd become freaks, too." That made you cry, you remember that. You remember hugging Bo, the way he smelled like cigarettes and hay. You ate three donuts, each one more stale than the last, but you couldn't seem to stop.

All the other details swirl into a too-bright fog through which you can't see clearly. Nothing remains, just a sour taste in your mouth when Poppy looks at you, a bad feeling that you can't quite shake.

The rest of the day goes perfectly smoothly, blurrily, quickly. You join the cheerleading squad and the student council. Everyone is kind. No one mentions the plane crash, or looks at you funny, or makes a comment about how you are white and Josh Harris is black. Your classes seem interesting. Your teachers kind. But even as you walk out of the building, thinking about what to tell your parents about your day when they ask, you already have started forgetting: It's like trying to hang on to a spider's web; the gossamer threads keep blowing farther away in a wind so slight that you can barely feel it on your skin.

*But I'm happy*, you think. *I'm happy.*

*This is happiness.*

*I am happy so everyone is happy.*

*I deserve to be happy.*

*Don't I?*

Your knuckles ache.

*"We would have been happy if we'd lived,"* say the stars.

*I'm not going crazy*, you tell yourself. *I will not go crazy. Not now. Not after everything that happened to get me to here. No one goes crazy in Wyoming. Right?*

Wyoming is your safe place.

# 25.

"WYOMING IS MY safe place," you'd said, and then you both laughed.

"Still?" Kath said.

"Oh, always," you said. "Once Wyoming, always Wyoming."

"You should get that on a T-shirt," she'd said.

Then: laughter.

*"Think of it like data storage. You can rewind or fast forward. It's all there. You just have to find it,"* says Dr. McDreamy in his soothing voice. You try to focus on his face, but it's like looking through a lens that's been smeared with Vaseline.

Rewind further:

You are lying on your back on a dock. The wood is old and smoothed out by time. In between each board, there is a gap of an inch or more, through which you can see the dark water of the lake. Kath's grandmother's summer place.

It's been a hot day and you are sunburned. Kath is not. "I feel sorry for you," she's saying. "It must be terrible to be a white person who turns so very, very pink."

"Ha ha," you're saying. "I hate you because you're beautiful." That's from an old ad from the 1980s. Kath is a collector of 1980s clothes, books, movies, ads. There is one pinned to her wall, a woman with long brown hair. "Don't hate me because I'm beautiful," it says in '80s font across her face, which makes it impossible not to hate her even though she's probably old now, not quite so loathsomely gorgeous.

Kath snort-laughs.

There is a storm coming. You can feel it prickling in the air: a heightened sense of something that is about to happen.

Something terrible.

Yet you don't move, neither of you do. You don't do the logical thing, which would be to get up, make your way up the long flight of stairs to the cabin, where the fireplace probably has been lit and one of her brothers is playing the piano or singing and someone is looking for a board game for everyone to play. Instead, you remain, bellies pressed to the wood, picking a splinter away from a board, watching a water beetle skittering across the lake through the gaps.

The evening sky, which was indigo blue and clean a few minutes ago, is becoming congealed with a thick black layer of clouds.

Kath is talking and talking. She is having a crisis. "Being in love is like having appendicitis," she is saying. "It hurts so much and then when it stops, you think you're better, but it turns out that you aren't better, your appendix has ruptured and you only have one good, pain-free day before it gets toxic in your blood and then sometimes you even die."

"Don't oversell love," you say, sarcastically. "I might want to fall into it one day."

"That's it!" she sits up straight, abruptly. You can see imprints of the boards on her skin. "That's why they say you *fall* into love! Because it's, like, terrifying. Think of something you can fall off or into that isn't scary. You can't! Right? So it's basically falling into the worst thing: love, quicksand. And you can't get out of it. The more you try, the more it drags you in. Then you're stuck and the sand goes over your face and you're trying to breathe in muck and you know you're going to die and then you do. That would be a terrible way to die, right? The worst thing I can think of."

"I think it would be worse to burn," you say, honestly. "Quicksand sounds like it would be soft and cool, at least."

"No way, it would be terrible," she says. "Anyway, it's a metaphor. The point is that love is stupid. Don't ever fall in love. But that's bad advice because you can't help it when it happens."

You don't tell her that you already are in love. You haven't fully confessed to her yet your feelings about Josh Harris. (It's always been Josh Harris. From fourth grade when he transferred into your school.)

From very very very far away you hear Josh Harris's voice, "Is it happening again, Schmidt? Would you like me to count?"

You nod, or try to. But you want to stay in the memory. There is something here that you need to see. That you want to remember.

You can hear him, slowly, thoughtfully, hitting each syllable individually, as though you are on a playground with a talking tube and he is in the north corner shouting into the end and you are in the south corner, pretending you can hear him. "One, two, three."

You turn your attention back to Kath on the dock. "Charlie is just so cute, right? And he's not like the other band losers. Plus, he can see that I'm pretty beyond the braces and stuff. Mom says you should always pick someone who can see beyond the immediate into your beautiful future."

"She *says* that?" you say. "That's weird. She talks like an inspirational cross-stitch."

Kath shrugs. "I agree with her. Fundamentally."

"Fundamentally!" You start laughing. Then you're both laughing, which is how it always is with you and Kath: hilarious.

The memory slides a bit, like a sheen of oil has covered it. You focus on it as hard as you can, holding on to it by clenching your hands. It works.

In the scene, it starts to rain. You remember that rain, how huge each drop was. Then, before you can even comment on the raindrops, the lightning starts forking down from the sky. It hits something—a pole?—at the end of the dock and the whole thing illuminates with a terrifying light that you can feel in your legs, the vibration of a current coming from who knows where. Your hair slowly rises up. So does Kath's.

"It's going to hit us," you say. You grab her hand and both of you are running. Her pulling you. You pulling her. The cabin is too far, so you duck into the haunted boat shack. You'd always called it that, daring each other to go inside, but never doing it. Her brothers used it as a clubhouse, but you'd never been in.

It smells like burlap and tar and paint. The rain hammers on the tin roof. You try not to think about lightning hitting that roof. It's pitch-black in there. Everywhere you touch feels like it's covered with cobwebs, thick with dust.

"Let's go to the house," you whisper. It doesn't seem right to talk in more than a whisper in here. Raising your voice would be wrong.

"Too far," she says. "We'll get hit by lightning. People don't survive that. I don't want to die. Not until I'm old."

"Where are you? I can't see you."

"I'm right here. How do you think you'll die?"

You shrug. "In an old folks' home? I'll choke on my mashed potatoes." Then, "I'm scared."

"Me too."

"What should we do?"

"Mom says that if you ever get scared, you should go to your happy place."

"Your happy place? What's that?"

"Like mine would be here. A place where you feel safe, no matter what. Then you, like, go there in your mind and then you start to feel like you're really there, so you feel safer. Mine is this place: Grandma's house. What would yours be?"

You think about it for a few seconds. Not the peach farm, where your parents are always bickering. Kath's house? You open your mouth. "Wyoming," you say.

"Wyoming!" she repeats. Then you're both shrieking, howling, repeating it over and over again. *Wyoming! WHY oh meeeee!* Screaming with laughter, giggling for so long and so hard that you don't even notice that the squall has passed.

The rain has stopped.

*Wyoming* was your inside joke.

"Are you back? Because we are very late for English class," says Josh Harris. His hand is resting on the top of your head. "We should go in."

"Sorry," you say. "I was just . . . Anyway, I'm fine now. I'm good. I'm sorry. I don't know what happened."

The thing is, if Wyoming was just a joke, how did you end up living here, for real?

*It's my safe place,* you remember yelling at your mom and dad. *I have to move there. It's the safe place.*

*"Don't get hysterical. It can still be your safe place. It's your safe place and our private joke. One thing can be both, you know. Two things can be true at the same time."*

"No, they can't," you tell her.

"Excuse me?" the teacher says. "Did you have something to add, Miss Schmidt? About *War and Peace*?"

"*War and Peace*?" you say.

"The book that we will be studying this term. It's quite famous. You may have heard of it." She laughs. "You seemed eager to say something. Have you read the book? Would you like to tell us about it?"

"Um," you say. "Well, I haven't read it." You sneak a glance at Josh Harris. "But I think it's about war? Then, a bunch of romance. And then at the end, there's peace."

"No spoilers." The teacher smiles. "I think you might be right. But let's find out, shall we?" She starts handing out copies. "Ultimately, you know, it's a love story. One character, a good man, loves another, a good woman. But then her goodness is tested. It becomes a philosophical question: When do people stop being good? It is indeed about a war, but it's mostly about people. I hope you like it because it will take a long time for us to get through." She approaches your row with the remaining pile of books. Each one is old and obviously has been read before. The one that you are given has half the cover torn off.

*Wa a Pea,* it says. You smile, even though you feel like crying.

Poppy, sitting next to you, leans over. "Your book is torn," she observes.

"Thank you, Captain Obvious," you reply, turning your body slightly away from her.

"No need to be so rude," she says. "You Americans."

You shrug. You know there's no point engaging her, but you don't know how you know there is no point. She's from England and you're from California. There isn't a possibility that your paths have crossed before.

Right?

*"You're seriously so dumb sometimes. Lovable, but dumb. Like a golden retriever. Remember that one we used to walk after school in third grade for a dollar? Old Rump? What a weird name for a dog. And man, those people were getting a good deal. Anyway, don't sweat*

*it. You'll figure it out. Just like scientists figured out that dinosaurs had feathers, so they were really just incredibly creepy and gigantic birds who died out because they were too ugly to continue to survive. Plus, the feathers were too feeble to be useful due to the fact that dinosaurs were the size of trucks and the feathers were not."*

"That makes no actual sense. You're starting to ramble," you say out loud. "Are you nervous?"

Without remembering how or when you left class, finished your day, packed your backpack, and drove home, you suddenly are *at* home, on the front steps, pushing open your front door and waving at Josh Harris, who beeps his horn cheerfully twice. So you aren't driving your truck, but you look around the side of the barn and it's still there. You walk over to it and open the driver's door. It looks clean. The keys are hanging on the visor.

"Soon," you tell it. "Just not yet. What if I forget how to drive while I'm doing it?"

From his paddock, Midi whinnies at the fence. "I'll be there soon, boy," you tell him. "We'll go look for the little people." Midi understands what you mean, always, even when you don't understand yourself.

That's the thing with animals, you think. They aren't unpredictable at all. Except for cats, which is why they are so scary. Josh Harris doesn't get it, and that makes you sad. Animals know what you're thinking, even before you know yourself.

Midi trots over to the barn. He knows you'll be back. He knows where you'll go. And he'll know to bring you back here, even if you lose your way.

Especially if you lose your way.

# 26.

You TRUDGE BACK through the dirt and gravel and mud to the front door of the house, kicking your shoes off this time so you don't track mud over your mom's carefully polished floors. The house always smells like wood soap and wax.

You forget about Poppy as soon as you get inside. And Kath. (Inasmuch as you can ever forget Kath. Which is impossible.) Rumpelstiltskin comes over, tail wagging, and licks your shoe energetically. "No licking, Rump," you tell him, rubbing his soft ears, letting him do it anyway. You bend over and sniff his head, breathing deeply. He smells like Orange Bunny, soft and safe and sleepy.

"Mom?" you call. "Dad?"

"We're in the kitchen!" Mom calls back.

You follow the sounds of music and the smell of cooking around the corner to the huge chef's kitchen, which came with the house. It's your dad's dream kitchen, based on some mash-up of cooking shows and *House Hunters*. Everywhere there is granite and subway tile, huge expanses of surfaces. It's as big as the garage in your old house.

The counter is covered with food in various stages of being chopped and diced. You think of the peach farm, with the chipped blue counters, the way the dishwasher door opened right into the island and you had to stand next to it to put dishes in. You feel a pang of homesickness.

"We're playing *Chopped*," says your dad. He's grinning from ear to ear. Even your mom looks happier than usual. "You're the judge."

"Are you two drunk? What is happening here?" You survey the mess, an open bottle of wine and two half-empty glasses, various things that look like candy and cheese curls and assorted vegetables all heaped in bowls. "Did you two have a simultaneous nervous breakdown while I was at school? This is all *very* weird."

"No, *so* much better than that," your mom giggles. "We've decided to share each others' interests. And your dad is interested in cooking. So we're preparing dishes with the same ingredients, and then you taste them and say who wins. That's a game he watches on TV. Whoever wins gets to decide what we do tomorrow."

"Wow," you say. "I was only gone for six hours. And aliens had time to land here and do their whole body-snatching thing and replace my real parents with happy people who do stuff together? Is this a thinly disguised cry for help?"

But it's hard not to get swept up in their good mood. "Oh, you have a doctor's appointment in thirty minutes," says your mom. "Dad will drive you so that I can get ahead with my Oreo-and-ghost-pepper flan."

"That sounds completely disgusting, by the way," you call, on your way up to your room to drop your stuff. You pause on the stairs. "A guy died in California during a burger eating contest when a ghost pepper ripped a hole in his throat. An actual hole! This weird dessert better not kill me."

You go up the rest of the stairs, dump your schoolbag on your bed, and go into the bathroom to wash your face. Your skin is completely, perfectly, dreamily clear. Your face has almost a luminous quality, a shimmer, like you've artfully applied highlighter, but you haven't. You aren't wearing any makeup. You reach up slowly and touch it. It's as smooth as silk.

It's possible that you've never looked this good, or maybe it's a symptom of only being able to see out of one eye. Or maybe the other eye is messed up, too, and is just making everything look better than it is, including you. Tentatively, you open your eye wide and touch the glass eye with your fingertip. It's as smooth as ice, a marble that looks like the planet Earth, all blues and greens and browns and white. A whole world there, where your eye used to be.

"Where I used to be," you whisper. Something hurts somewhere. It's your stomach or your chest, like a bruise being pushed hard. "Who are you?" Then, "Don't get crazy." You stick out your tongue at yourself. "Crazier," you amend.

You let the hot water run over your hands for a minute, then two. The heat feels nice. Your Junky Idiotic Arthritis hasn't been bad all summer, now that you think about it, but suddenly—it must be because the weather is changing, autumn has crept up on you—it throbs. The dampness in the air is inside you somehow, making your knuckles ache. The feeling is like when you have cramps with your period, a pain that you manage to completely obliterate from your memory in the four or so weeks between periods, but then when it starts again, it's so crushingly and depressingly familiar, so oh-*this*-again, you want to cry. You flex your fingers a few times. You'll have to dig out the paraffin bath from wherever you unpacked it.

The thing is, you don't remember unpacking it.

You don't even remember packing it.

You sit down on the edge of the bathtub, staring at your hands. When was the last time you used it? California? You don't remember ever seeing it here. On the other hand, you also don't recognize the shoes that you're wearing, Converse decorated with a pattern of the galaxy. They look new.

"It's getting worse," you acknowledge out loud. "It's getting *bad*."

Your voice is absorbed by the plants, the greenness of them, which suddenly reminds you exactly of the sunroom at Kath's house, where her mom grew orchids, hidden among all the vines. You pick up a leaf from the closest plant. "I am the leaf," you whisper. Leaves are never scared. So why do you feel scared?

"*I do not fear death,*" says the leaf.

The leaf is dark green but pink-veined; you crumple it between your fingers, tearing it into bits.

Kath's mom shimmers into your memory. "That's a nerve plant," she says. "One of my favorites. And it won't kill the cats if they eat it, and they eat it all the time. Nontoxic. It's a good quality in a houseplant." Something brushes by your leg: a brown cat, spotted, moving fast. You reach down for it before you realize that it isn't there.

You sneeze once, twice, three times.

"This isn't good," you say out loud. You can't start imagining cats. That would be crazy. Where is the line between sane and insane?

You have a feeling that you keep moving it, inch by inch.

Because you're *happy*.

You *are*.

You are happy and you are going to hold on to that happiness with your aching hands for as long as you can. You flex your fingers again.

From downstairs you hear your dad calling you. "We'll be late, hon! Step it up! Dr. McDreamy is waiting."

"I'll be right there!" you call. "I just need to grab something."

You go through your closet and into your secret room. You reach out and touch the peach scarf, hanging in the window. The autumn sun is filtering through, a more faded sun than it has been all summer, more watery. Cooler. You take the scarf down. The colors are as vibrant as the day you bought it; it's been undamaged by the sun. You press it against your nose, like maybe you'll be able to smell Paris, but it smells like *you*, shampoo and something sweet, coconut and vanilla. You wind it around your thumb once, twice, three times. You watch the skin on your thumb turn white, then start to go purple.

Josh Harris was sleeping on the plane.

You were drawing in your sketchpad.

The yellow masks dropped.

"Pith you, Schmidt," Kath said.

The room tilts, just like the plane did. You lean over for a minute, bent double, until it rights itself again.

You go to the desk and open the drawer under the shelf where the mason jars hold your collection of pens: rows and rows of black pens, organized by thickness of the nib. You haven't drawn anything in so long. When did you last draw? You pick up a pen and hold it. The weight of it feels unfamiliar in your hand.

You haven't.

Not once.

Not since *Before*.

You frown. You look around the nook that you've set up. You did this, didn't you? It looks like something you would have done. It couldn't possibly have just been here, waiting for you, with all your things. Your heart thuds hard against your breastbone.

*"HEY," says Mr. Appleby.*

You look down at your hand, expecting the pen, but your hand is holding your sketchpad: *ME AND JOSH HARRIS: A LOVE STORY*, your favorite pen tucked into the coil.

216

Well, no, it's not. It can't be.

That would be ridiculous.

It burned in the plane. You did not take it with you when you rolled. It wouldn't have been possible. Your empty hands, grabbing at the gravelly mountainside while you rolled rolled rolled.

You're hallucinating or dreaming or both. You rifle through the pages in the sketchbook and they are all there. You fight the urge to scream.

"It is what it is," you say. "Is what it is what it is?" Your heart is going too fast now. You sit down. Kath used to hate it when you said that.

"It's just a completely redundant phrase," she'd say. "Everything *is* what it *is*. You know which other phrase I hate? 'Everything's cracked, or else the light couldn't get in.'"

"I don't think that's a phrase. Isn't it a line in a song or something?"

"It's a phrase. Trust me. And it's stupid. Because obviously not everything is cracked. Some things are just dark."

"Kath?" you say now, out loud. You hesitate, and then you stuff *ME AND JOSH HARRIS: A LOVE STORY*, which can't exist, but does, into your bag. You stand up.

Your brain makes the jangling keys sound. It can't be the same sketchpad; it is the same sketchpad. Two truths. Something is a lie.

But which one is the lie?

Your sketchpad burned when the fuel tanks on the crashed plane ignited, sending a fireball ricocheting down the side of the mountain in France.

Right?

You have to show it to Dr. McDreamy.

You have to *demand an explanation*.

You will say, "This can't be real." You will say it with *intent*, a word that is quickly losing its meaning to you.

*Intent* (n.): intention or purpose; something that is intended, chosen. An act of choice, intention, decision.

*Intent* (adj.): the bridge between choice and action.

Choice, choice, choice.

Intent is choice.

*Life or death?*

*CHOOSE.*

Tears come from both your eyes—a glass eye can, after all, still produce tears. Who knew?

"Everything is a choice," you whisper.

You imagine that Dr. McDreamy will be comforting. He will look at the sketchbook and he will understand. He will say something in his low, dulcet voice: *"Touch, feel, see, smell, anchor yourself and you'll be well."* He'll take the sketchpad from your hand, holding it in such a way that you can't see what is inside, what would be impossible to have inside it. He will solve the mystery by erasing the mystery with *intent* and everything will get better again and you can preserve your happiness, which right now is feeling as fragile as splintering glass, shattering ice.

*"What is your intent?"* he'll say, looking at your eyes. *"Believe in your power to intend."*

"*Intend* is one of those words that, when repeated, begins

to be meaningless," you'll say. "I intend to tend the tent with intent."

You laugh. Everything is funny. Nothing is funny.

*Something is very wrong here.*

*Choose.*

Dr. McDreamy might be a good person to deliver the news to your parents. He has such an understanding face. He's very good at that. You know he is. You've seen it on TV.

But still, you might not show it to him yet.

You might not quite be ready.

"I love you," you tell Orange Bunny, holding him briefly to your nose. You inhale and hold a breath of him in. "You're my safe place," you tell him. "We've got this. What's a little head injury, anyway? *Traumatic brain insult.* People survive worse."

Orange Bunny's neck flops listlessly to the side.

You put him carefully back down on the shelf, resting him next to your phone charger, and a pile of books you haven't touched since you moved in. *War and Peace* is on the top. But how did it get there already? Wasn't that just handed out in class today?

Half of its cover missing. *Wa a Pea,* you think, frowning. *Wa a Pea.*

Your missing eye is hurting, the ghost of the pain that took it.

A memory struggles to surface, like someone fighting against quicksand, kicking hard to try to get to the surface for just one more gasp of air.

part **three**

# 27.

You are riding Midi, hard.

It's drizzling rain and a wind is whipping through the stand of birch trees that you're passing through, the yellowing leaves falling like golden flakes of snow. Midi's hooves are thundering against the path, which is cut through the knee-deep wild grasses and flowers. The vibration is jarring your teeth in your jaw, making your legs ache and your hips burn, but you keep going. The air is rich with the mulchy smell of fall.

What month is it?

You have lost some time.

How much time have you lost?

How much time can you lose if you've lost all the time that you had?

*"How much wood would a woodchuck chuck if a woodchuck could chuck wood?"*

Last night, you stayed up late, Googling "time." "Time is just a construct," it said, "that allows us to feel like we have some control over that which we can't control." You have no idea what that means but you also do, because you know that you have no control over anything. As if to agree with you, Midi throws his head back, nearly taking you out.

"Hey," you say, ineffectively.

You keep firm hold on the reins but glance down at what you're wearing: jeans, boots, layers of sweaters, a puffy down jacket. Your socks, peeking out over the top of the boots, are orange and black striped. Halloween? Is it *October*?

Have you lost a whole month?

And anyway, why are you galloping? You feel an impetus to hurry, but why?

You grit your teeth, clench your jaw, try to find your way to where you are. Your thinking is getting murkier, that's the problem. It's all confusion and you don't know what to do about it. Up ahead through the trees, you see another rider on a horse, galloping fast. *Thundering*, you think. A boy, you can tell from the shape of him, so it must be Josh Harris. Loving Josh Harris is the one thing that you are sure of, even when everything else is slipping away. You watch as the horse clears a fallen tree gracefully.

"But Josh Harris doesn't ride," you say to Midi. "Josh Harris is afraid of horses."

A hazy image swims into view, but this isn't your memory, it's his, a story that he read out loud in English class,

*Before*: a county fair, riding a pony, the pony throwing him and then rearing, his front hoof coming down inches from Josh Harris's neck.

When you asked him if he'd ride with you now, he said, "I can't trust an animal who is that large and yet so totally submissive to people sitting on him and kicking him in the side."

"You allow *me* to sit on you," you'd said, and then you'd done just that.

Then you didn't need to talk any more.

*Lips like velvet.* What would Kath say now?

*"I wouldn't say anything, duh. For one thing, that would be the* most *awkward thing of all time, talking to you while you're actively making out. For another thing, I'm running out of things to say on the topic of Just Josh."*

Midi slows, bucking, and arches his back. "Whoa," you say. "Whoa there."

You rub his neck, easing him up. He slows to a trot. He's out of breath, but so are you. Riding is more work than it looks.

"Take it easy," you whisper to yourself, to him. Gradually, he stops flicking his ears, and he settles into a walk. You feel your own pulse slow to match his stride. In the trees, small birds are whistling and chirping. Every once in a while, one flutters from one branch to the next, disappearing into the foliage, the sudden flurry of his wings startling you.

Midi's sides gradually stop heaving. He's sweating. You wipe his damp neck. Now that you've slowed down, your hands are instantly cold, the ache from the chill cutting into your joints as swiftly as blades. Why aren't you wearing gloves? Your skin is red and looks chapped from the chill and the wind. A manicure is mostly chipped away, but looks like it was dark blue.

There is a ringing in your ears.

You are on a narrow, cobbled street in Paris. A manicurist on the corner, a row of women leaning over small tables, painting the nails of casually sophisticated French women and a couple of obvious American tourists. "Let's do it," said Kath. "My treat."

Once inside, you're nearly overwhelmed by the smell of chemicals. The manicurist soaks your hand in a hot bath and massages your knuckles. It's heaven, like your wax bath at home, but better. Paris is so damp and the junky idiotic pain tries to cling on to you like a crab with claws, but her firm stroke gently eases it away. Kath chooses the color for you. It's called "Schoolboy Blazer," you remember that. "I don't know why, but I feel like you'd like a schoolboy in a blazer, a private school fancy guy with all those extra manners and who wears a tie."

"I'd consider it if Josh Harris was the boy in question," you say.

"Your loyalty is totally adorable. Not sure he's worthy of it, but whatever. You do you."

The polish is blue.

Dark blue.

Your hands are holding the reins of a white horse and you are in the woods and the wind is pushing the leaves this way and that and the path is gravel and dust is kicked up by the horse's hooves in clouds and you're coughing and coughing.

Why are your nails still Schoolboy Blazer blue?

When did you—?

You drop the reins, letting Midi take you wherever he wants to go, stuffing your hands into your sleeves so you can't see your nails, hoping to warm your throbbing knuckles. You pass a tree hung with shoes but then when you look closer this time, you realize it's a flock of crows, rising into the sky, loudly.

You try to organize your thoughts or at least get hold of them, which is like trying to grab a handful of fish out of the sea: They keep slipping through your fingers, silvering away in the beams of sunlight coming through the surface. You look up at the sun. It's sitting high in the sky, mostly behind veils of damp gray clouds, but still white-bright, starlight, trying to burn through. You guess that it is afternoon. It must be a weekend. So say it's a weekend in October then.

What have you missed?

Who is that boy?

You recognize the path as the one that leads up the side of the mountain. From the uppermost part of the trail, you can branch right to go to the lake or left to go to a viewing spot where you can see the Greater Green River Intergalactic Spaceport. You know *that*, but you don't know what month it is, you don't know who is on the other horse, you don't really remember anything beyond the first days of school, getting into your dad's car to go see Dr. McDreamy, your sketchbook stuffed into your bag, just in case.

"When are you going to start driving that shiny red truck?" he'd said.

You didn't know how to tell him that you couldn't, just in case you forgot how when you were pulling out onto the highway, the river of cars drowning you while you sat, stalled, unsure of how to make it go.

"*There* you are!" A boy's voice pulls you out of your reverie. He pulls his horse up. He's panting and his horse's sides are heaving. The horse is gray, dappled, a longer dark mane. He looks like a living version of a plastic horse that used to sit on your windowsill when you were little.

"Oh, he's so beautiful," you say.

"Yes, well. He is rather nice, I know. But what happened to you, Pixie? Thought you were a good enough rider to keep up."

"And I thought you didn't ride."

"Why would you think that? That's a bit mad. We do this every weekend. Ohhhh, wait a minute. This is one of those things, right? Where you *glitch*. Traumatic head injury. Don't worry. It happens."

"Oh," you say. "I—"

"Do I have to explain the whole thing again, about how you and I are secretly in love, although you persist in seeing that terribly good-looking Josh-person and acting as though our love is just a figment of my imagination?"

You roll your eyes. "I'm *so* sure that's an accurate portrayal of the reason why we are riding horses up the mountain and freezing to death in the process."

"I told you to wear gloves," he says.

228

"Well, if you did, I don't remember, so it doesn't matter, I'm still cold. Let's go back."

"But you promised to show me the mysterious Jupe landing strip! Where all those poor, displaced Jupiterians decide that Wyoming is the only place they can go, after an asteroid smashed into their own planet in, what did you say? 1994? Taking their bloody time getting here, aren't they?"

"Do you always talk in paragraphs? It's exhausting."

"Yes, I do, and you like it. Hmmm. I rather enjoy this, actually, you not remembering. Makes things easier."

"That sounded both incredibly creepy *and* incredibly threatening. Nice combination. You should consider selling that as a marketing campaign to McDonald's or something. Big Mac: Now both creepy AND threatening. Enjoy one today!" You turn Midi around. "I think we'll go ahead and turn back."

"Oh, come on, don't be like that. I was just taking the piss," he says.

"Do English people really say that? Of all the things that came from England, that's one of the worst. That *word*. Ugh."

"Which word? Taking? Terrible, isn't it? Can't think why I get away with it."

"Oh, ha ha. You're very funny. So funny, I forgot to laugh. Which, by the way, isn't something I've said since I was nine. You bring out the nine-year-old in me, and that is not a good thing." You feel in your back pocket for your phone. Not there. You pat your coat pockets, finding a granola bar and a bottle of water, but still no phone. You unwrap the granola bar and eat it. It tastes stale. You rewrap the remainder and put it back in your pocket. You wonder if the jacket is even yours. You're not sure it looks like something you would choose. On the other hand, it does look like something someone in Wyoming would wear. Or someone in an ad for L.L.Bean.

"Oh pleeeeeeeeeease take me to the Jupiter Airport. I promise that if a spaceship lands, I'll get directly on it and be gone on the next shuttle to the homeland."

"England?"

"No, silly, play along. I meant *Jupiter*. Now let's go to the creek and let these poor horses drink before they drop dead."

You follow him, rubbing Midi's neck. The horses wade right into the creek, which is more like a river than when you last saw it. The water rushes around their knees.

"Now this is more like it, Pixie," says Benedict Cumberbatch. "Ideal. A pretty girl. A pretty river. Pretty fall colors, et cetera. *Very* pretty, all of it."

"I have a boyfriend. I haven't forgotten that."

"Right, right, I know. He's very tall. And you'd never consider me to be a contender anyway, because, how did you put it, I'm too snively? Did you say snively? That doesn't sound like a very American thing to say."

"I can say without a shadow of a doubt that I never said you were *snively*. I don't even know what it means. That your nose is drippy? You are a bit of a drip. Maybe I said you were drippy, but even that seems more like something you would say than something I would say."

*"Benedict Cumberbatch looks like a snively weasel. It's one hundred percent implausible that Emma Stone would fall for him so exuberantly. She is a kick-ass woman and he is a worm."*

230

"I may have said *wormy*," you say.

"Drippy is definitely an English thing. And, compared to wormy—which is terribly rude, by the way, unless you're talking about a dog—it's downright complimentary. I'll take drippy." He wipes his nose on his sleeve. "Although I'm also snively right now. We also say wet. If you were English, you'd say that you can't fall in love with me because I'm too *wet*."

You look at him, dubiously. "Are you *wet*?"

"No, I'm not even damp. See what I did there? You're enjoying this, aren't you?"

"Not even a little bit. I'm faking it. I'm confused, mostly. But as you know, I had a head injury. Dr. . . ." Your brain goes blank again on the name, but you forge ahead. "Dr. McDreamy says that when you have a traumatic brain insult, your memories are in files and you have to, you have to, you have to . . . Oh, forget it. I don't know right now. Sometimes things get . . . hazy."

"I hate to say it, but 'hazy' sounds concerning. Have you told your doctor? Very odd name, he has, by the way. Not sure that's a real name. He might be a fraud."

"I don't know," you say, suddenly starting to laugh. "I don't remember if I've told him or not."

He laughs, too. "Of course you don't."

You laugh and laugh and laugh for so long that your belly aches and tears streak down your cheeks. It feels so good to laugh like that. It feels like the point. It makes you think of Kath. You don't even know any girls in Wyoming, except Poppy, you guess, but she is neither funny nor your friend. Just thinking about her makes you feel queasy in a Pavlovian way.

Something about her once made you throw up.

A rush of saliva fills your mouth.

"Okay, you're laughing. Good. That's good. But does it mean you'll show me where the aliens will land when they arrive?" he says.

"Fine, fine," you say. "Yes. You've won me over with the laughing. But not in an 'I want to make out with you' way. Only in a 'we are sort of friends, I guess' way. So don't get excited."

"Too late. I am already ninety-two percent excited."

"Well, settle down to something in the low forties. Let's ride."

He nudges his horse into a slow walk and you keep talking. "Did I ever tell you that somewhere in these mountains, they found mummies of tiny people? Like, a foot tall. They weren't babies, they were actual adult humans. Maybe they built the Jupiter landing strip here because the Jupes were already here! Little tiny Jupes." You snort with laughter.

"Hmm, what was that Dr. McDreamy said? Traumatic brain insult?"

You have to give Midi a kick to get him going. "No, I'm serious! Before the crash, I did a huge project about Wyoming. It was called: *Wyoming: Weird and Wild.* I think I even won some kind of prize for it. I remember a slide show and having to talk in front of the school. Anyway, it had all these fun facts." You close your eyes, remembering. Midi keeps walking, following Dwayne's horse. You can remember exactly what you were wearing: a hoodie that said, WYOMING: THE EQUALITY STATE. Their motto is actually "Equal rights," which, now that you think about it, is why you picked it in the first place. "I can't remember what I did last Monday, but I can remember that tiny mummies were found in the San Pedro Mountains and that they were called 'the little people' but now that I've said that out loud, I'm wondering if I'm remembering wrong, because wouldn't that be a huge deal?"

"Uh, yeah. Tiny mummy people? Def a huge deal."

"Right, so maybe I'm wrong. But I think I'm not wrong. I'm pretty sure I remember it."

"What else do you remember?"

"Well, from that same assignment, I remember a guy named Big Nose George, who was basically a bad guy, robbing stagecoaches and maybe killing people. I forget that part. After they hung him for his crimes, they took all the skin off his body and made it into a doctor's bag and, I *think*, a pair of shoes."

"That is a *truly* repulsive story. Thank you so much for sharing it with me. Now I will always remember it and I will likely never sleep again."

"Well, sorry. But you asked."

"I'm taking the piss again. Although I am inclined towards nightmares."

"You and Josh Harris, both," you say, without meaning to break a confidence, it just slips out. "You two should be friends."

He shakes his head and turns around in the saddle to face you. "We can't possibly be friends! We're both vying for the heart of the same lovely maiden."

You roll your eye. "That's ridiculous. You can't vie for my heart. My heart is unviable."

"Unviable! Tragic. That means you'll be dead soon and we should snog immediately before it's too late. If I snog you after you're dead, I believe it's a crime."

"Snog! That's another terrible British word. It's an unforgivable word. I'm never going to kiss an English person now, not ever, because they might describe it using that word and then I'll have to kill them."

"And make their skin into a doctor's bag?"

"Nope, just a regular purse. Or maybe gloves. My hands are so cold."

"Here, wear my gloves." He takes them off and tosses them back to you, one by one. You don't argue. Your hands are already resisting bending. You put them on, feeling where they are already warm from his hands. You blush. There's something too intimate about the gloves but you are so desperate for the warmth you can't exactly refuse them.

"You're welcome," he calls.

"Thanks! It's just that I have this arthritis. My hands get—"

"I know," he interrupts. "Pretend I already know everything about you, because I do. I collect facts about you, Elyse Schmidt. Like you collect facts about weird ways to die, and Wyoming, especially weird ways to die IN Wyoming. For the record, I am fourteen percent in love with you."

"I thought it was seven, at last count. What changed?"

"It's gone up since we started this ride. I don't even like horses, or even if I did, I'd never admit it because it would make my dad too happy. *Not* pleasing my dad is my primary interest and you, my brain-injured manic pixie girl, are my secondary interest."

"You're veering into creepy territory again. Maybe more riding and less talking."

"But I have more things to say."

"I don't. I'm on a break."

"You don't just go on a break from a conversation. That's not normal. Also, I'm no etiquette expert, but I suspect that it's rude."

"Well, then I'm rude. I'm okay with that. Deal." You close your good eye for a second, letting Midi rock you gently as he steps carefully up the now-gravelly trail. Your glass eye feels wet, but you touch it and it's the same as always: cool, unyielding, smooth. You blink, hard. Midi slips a little, scrambling to not lose his footing. The trail is getting steeper. You need to concentrate.

"I thought you didn't know the way!" you call.

He raises his hand. "No talking! You're on a break!"

"You can't see it, but I'm rolling my eye," you tell his receding back, nudging Midi to keep up. "I'm rolling it so hard I may cause it permanent damage. And it's not like I have an eye to spare. Without it, I'll be fully blind. But don't let the guilt eat away at you."

You let him get farther ahead. It's better that way.

You miss Josh Harris.

Where is he?

How does he feel about you riding off with Benedict Cumberbatch?

Did you fight?

*Pow pow*, Josh Harris would say, which is as close as he comes to bantering.

But he isn't here.

You have no one to ask.

# 28.

THE SIDE OF the path offers a steep drop-off, which is giving you vertigo. The third most common cause of death by selfie is people wanting to show off how close to the edge they were willing to go, and then falling off. You got really good at drawing those people, posing on top of buildings, and then just their feet in the next frame as they toppled over the side. You frown. How could you have found it funny? They died, all those people. They were real. But somehow they didn't seem real. Not quite. They were more like characters playing a part in this ongoing movie of the internet.

Now that you think of it, you feel sorry for all of them, but not as sorry as you feel for the woman who was hiking at the Grand Canyon and stepped aside on the path to let someone else pass, lost her footing, and plunged to her death.

"The thing is," you tell Midi. "We're all just one side step away from being dead." He snorts.

"You sound like Kath," you tell him. "I miss her so much." You lean forward and rest your head on Midi's neck.

It is raining again now. What began as a drizzle has quickly developed into an actual downpour. You urge Midi on, straightening up in the saddle, keeping him away from slippery edges.

You ride alone for ages. You almost forget that you're here with Benedict Cumberbatch, when you catch up with him by the lake. It's a beautiful lake—like a postcard—and it seems to appear so suddenly through the trees, like something magical. It makes you gasp every time you see it, blue-green and still. Today, it's darker than usual, reflecting the now-hostile sky.

You want to flip the image over, write *WISH YOU WERE HERE*, and mail the whole thing to Kath.

Not possible, you remind yourself. Not a postcard. No address, even if it were.

The lake stretches perfectly mountain blue-green into the distance, necklaced by trees in all different shades of autumn.

"This is gorgeous," Benedict Cumberbatch says. "It *almost* makes me like Wyoming, but don't tell my father. I don't think we should go any farther because it's getting too slippery, but I realize now that I see this lake that this was fate. To heck with Jupiter! This lake is a jewel. This lake is the best thing about Wyoming, other than you. Look at the color of it. It is the most romantic spot on the planet."

"Well, I wouldn't go that far. It's very pretty, though," you agree. You look up at the sky, which is darkening. "But lakes and lightning storms aren't a good mix."

"No, I suppose they—" His words are cut off when the lightning forks down in a huge arc of brilliant white light. You watch like you're paralyzed, like you have no choice. The light is blinding. Once, twice, three times, pelting noisily into the lake, bolts of vibrating whiteness that seem to turn the surface water briefly purple. You can feel Midi tensing, like he's about to bolt, shifting on his feet.

"SHELTER," you both say at once. You pull the horses around and gallop toward a trail shelter, not quite going all out, but as close as it is safe to go. You dismount at the shed and try to calm Midi by whispering in his ear. His eyes roll. He wants to run, you can feel it. You understand it.

*Escape, escape, escape.*

But if you let him go, then you'll be trapped, too. You lash him onto the lashing post.

"This was pretty dumb," you say. "We should have checked the weather forecast. I've been almost hit by lightning before—"

But before you can even finish your sentence, suddenly he's in front of you and then you're *kissing* him, or he's kissing you and you aren't trying to stop him, because he's Benedict Cumberbatch and he's your free pass.

*"Uh, that was a deal you made with me, not with Just Josh Harris."* But you're not listening to Kath because you lived and you're alive and you're happy and you're kissing Benedict

Cumberbatch for all the stars in the sky, it's your job to do that, to do everything because you survived and so you have to kiss the boys and make the mistakes and dodge the lightning bolts and keep going and keep going and keep going even when you don't know why or how or what.

You're *not* a bad person.

You just have to do it.

To do *this*.

For all of the two hundred and sixteen people on the plane who didn't live.

"Poppy's never going to believe this," he says, when you both pull away, out of breath. The rain has slowed to a drizzle now. The air is still and cool and it's so quiet that it's impossible to believe that there ever was lightning and you can hear your own heart beating and your lips are sore in a good way.

"If you tell her, I'll make you into a purse," you say. A bird flies past, low and loud, making a noise that sounds like screaming. You stop laughing and just like that, the moment has passed, the moment where this made sense, the moment where it felt right.

What is *wrong* with you?

You push away from Benedict Cumberbatch and half walk, half stumble back to Midi, who tries to nuzzle your shoulder. You untether him and get back into the saddle in one fast motion, kicking him into a fast trot, as fast as it's safe to go on the slippery downhill trail. You don't wait for *Dwayne*.

What kind of name is that anyway?

You pretend you can't hear him yelling behind you, "Wait for me, Pixie! Was it something I said?"

# 29.

IT IS NOVEMBER.

The leaves are mostly gone from the trees and seeing their bare bones makes you anxious. Worse, there is something wrong with Rumpelstiltskin. He won't get up without your mom or dad lifting him. He no longer licks your shoes. He looks different somehow: If a dog can look pale, he's managed it. Your mom and dad are devastated, weepy, bereft. It seems strange to you; they've only known him for a few months. Still, they move around the house as quietly as ghosts, hushed as though they are already deeply in mourning.

You are in your room.

Rain is hitting the skylight sideways. It might be snow. Or even sleet.

You are wearing a strapless dress with huge ruffles. It's ugly. No matter which angle you look at yourself from, you look ridiculous. The problem is that you can't remember why you are wearing it. It is pink. Really pink. You are not a pink person.

"Pretty in Pink. *Remember? We watched it thirteen times in a row on my thirteenth birthday and then we went crazy-bananas from lack of sleep and I cut your hair to look like Molly Ringwald's? You looked like her. Except, you know. Shorter. And brunettier."*

"I remember the dumb movie and the bad haircut," you say. "I'm kind of hazy about why I'm wearing the dress right now, though. I remember being brunette. That was another life, though. Not this one."

*"Hey, it's your story. You drew it. Don't ask me."*

"What?" Your heart stops beating cold in your chest. You cough. "What? Kath?"

"Did you say something, honey?" Your mom peeks around your door. "Oh, you look so pretty! Well, as pretty as someone can look in a hideous 1980s dress. When I was your age, we all wore those, obviously, but we knew they were terrible, even back then. I never would have believed that these eighties-themed dances would be a thing! Who wants to wear flammable fabric and look dumpy on purpose? And the hair! I mean, you did a great job, but it's terrible."

"Wow, you are doing wonders for my self-esteem. Thanks for dropping by, Mom."

"Oh, honey, you look fine. You always look beautiful. I'm sorry."

"*Fine* is what I was shooting for, I'm almost sure of it. So thank you."

"Are you almost ready? Because Josh is here."

"Josh Harris," you correct her.

"Do you know any other Joshes?" she asks.

"MOM, it's just his name, okay?"

"Like how he calls you Schmidt?"

"I guess. But I wish he wouldn't."

"Maybe he wishes you wouldn't call him Josh Harris. It's so—" She wrinkles her nose. "It's so formal. You two have been dating for so long now. Maybe time to move on to first names?"

"We're not ready to take such a huge step," you tell her. "Don't ruin my innocence."

"Oh, speaking of innocence. I think it's probably time that we talked about birth control, things like that. I know you don't want to, I just think—"

"MOM, we use condoms, okay?"

"You're already having sex with Josh?"

"JOSH HARRIS! And yes. I mean, we have. Once. I think. I mean, once that I— Oh, Mom, please don't make me talk to you about this."

"I'm not *making* you. But I'm your mother. I thought we were best friends. How was it?"

"Are you asking me how sex was with my boyfriend? Isn't that way too personal?"

"I don't know! I've never had a daughter before who is having sex with her boyfriend. This is a first for me, too.

Everything you go through, all your stages and phases, all firsts for me." She looks so sad, you want to hug her.

"It's fine, Mom. I'm sorry. It was fine. It was nice. I mean, I think it was good. It was. It was everything I wanted my first time to be."

"But what about the second time?"

"I think we haven't . . . I mean, we didn't . . . I don't know. It was the first time that was important. I wanted the first time to be with Josh Harris and it was and then—"

You blink, because suddenly there are tears in your good eye and it's hard to see your mom, where she's sitting on the edge of your perfectly made bed. It's like there is Vaseline on the lens. "Don't be sad, Mom. I'm sorry. It was perfect. It was a perfect first time."

She smiles, but she still looks funny, like she's on the verge of tears. "It goes by so fast," she says. "And then it's gone."

"Okay, you're really starting to make me sad, Mom. Please don't. Seriously. I'm going to a dance! It's supposed to be fun."

"Is there anything else you want to talk about? I want to hear all your things. I feel like we don't talk anymore. How's school? Have you made friends?"

You feel a wave of something, like you're going to either throw up or faint, you aren't sure which. "Mom," you say. "You know."

"I don't know! How would I know?"

"Don't shout at me!"

244

"I'm not shouting! You're shouting! Keep your voice down! Josh will wonder what's going on!"

"Mom, is he here? Downstairs? Right now? Is there any percent chance that he can hear this conversation?"

"Well, I suppose so. If he has very good hearing."

"Josh Harris *does* have very good hearing," you hiss in a whisper. "He does. His hearing is basically super human! He probably heard all this!"

"I'm sorry, Elyse," she stage whispers, flecks of spit landing on your glasses. "Kiss him, and then he'll forget."

"That's such an un-Mom thing to say."

"Is it?" she smiles. "Kiss him, you fool!"

"Mom!"

"I just love you so much, Elyse."

"I know you do, Mom. I love you, too."

"I really love you."

"Okay, this is getting weird, Mom. But I really love you, too."

"I love you forever. To the moon and back."

"Me too, Mom. Can I go downstairs now? Josh Harris is waiting."

Your mom grabs you in her arms. "I just never want to let you go," she says. "I never want you to leave. Remember when you were little? There was a poem I used to read to you. It had this one line, 'I carry your heart (I carry it in my heart).' And then one day, you drew it for me on a card. Me, carrying my own heart like a suitcase, with your heart inside it. I still have that card. I look at it every day."

"I'm going to a dance, Mom. Not Jupiter. Why are you crying?"

"I'm not crying," she says, crying harder.

"Okay, I *really* have to go. Are you going to be normal when I get back?"

She holds up one hand. "I'm going to be okay. I have to keep going."

"Good. This has been very weird."

"Have fun. Promise me that you'll be happy, wherever you go, whatever happens."

"Fine, I will. But not because this isn't the strangest send-off of all time."

"Goodbye, my Elyse, my small heart."

"Bye, Mom. Tell Dad I love him and I'll see him later."

"He knows." She chokes on a sob.

"MOM," you say.

She waves her hand at you. "It's fine," she says. "Enjoy Paris."

"Paris? Mom, I'm going to a dance."

Then everything goes prickly and then white and you're falling, you're falling, you're falling and you are falling and . . .

*What the actual fuck?* you think.

# 30.

Josh Harris is on the porch when you go down to the front door. Rumpelstiltskin thumps his tail when you walk by, your heels clicking on the wood floor.

*"We had to stop walking Ol' Rump because he got off the leash that time and he got into grocery store and jumped right into the meat freezer. I think the owners had to pay like three hundred dollars for the damage to all the meat, but he was just so happy. We couldn't get him out. I mean, we could have, but it would have been mean. Do you remember? Do you remember all of it? Everything?"*

"Yes," you say. "No." You frown. You stand in the hallway of this strange new house in Wyoming and you turn around and look at the walls, which are all painted white. The white is too bright and it hurts your good eye. There are framed photos lining the walls. You and Kath in third grade. You and Kath at a Girl Guide camp. You and Kath at a party. You and Kath standing under a rainbow of droplets in a waterfall somewhere. You and Kath at sunset on the beach, making a heart with your hands. You and Kath and you and Kath and you and Kath.

"All my memories are you," you say.

*"Look what you've done, though,"* she says. *"This is pretty amazing, Nerdball. All of this. Wyoming. You should have started that YouTube channel. You'd have a million subscribers! Your drawing is magic, obviously."*

"My drawing," you repeat, dully. You look down at your hand. For your whole life, your middle finger has been stained with black ink from holding the pen, calloused from the way you grip too hard. But now it is clean and smooth. It doesn't look like your hand at all.

"Who are you?" you ask yourself. "What have you done?"

You feel strange, like that time when you were in kindergarten and you got a fever so high that you passed out in the classroom, falling right down onto the hopscotch rug. You woke up looking at Mrs. Waterfield's shoes but they weren't shoes at all; in your fever dream they were fish, huge salmon, their mouths open, laughing at you.

You feel like that now.

You could open the door and anything could be there.

A salmon. Death. A unicorn. Who knows?

What would you draw, if you were going to draw it?

You open the door. Josh Harris looks at you and his eyes are wide, as though you, Elyse Schmidt, are the most beautiful girl he has ever seen. "Schmidt," he says. "You look amazing."

He holds out a corsage. The corsage is one perfect purple flower.

"Put it on me," you say, and he pins it carefully to your dress. You almost want him to stab you with the pin, so you know you can feel something. You press your head against his shoulder. "Thanks," you say, into his armpit. He's wearing something ridiculous: a powder-blue tuxedo.

Of course he is.

You knew he would be.

In the paddock, Midi rears up in the moonlight. For some reason, wind is blowing and his mane shimmers. "Your horse looks like a unicorn," Josh Harris says.

"Are you afraid?" you ask him.

He shakes his head. "I do not fear death," he says.

"I meant of unicorns. Are you afraid of unicorns?" You shiver. You're so cold, but also sweating.

Josh Harris throws back his head and laughs. "No way," he says. "I'm not scared, Schmidt." He offers his arm and you take it, walking carefully so you don't trip over the bottom of the long dress, so you don't stumble on the path in your heels. He's holding on to your arm too hard. You don't know how to tell him. *You're going to break my arm* is on the tip of your tongue but you don't say it.

Josh Harris can break your arm if he needs to, whatever he needs, you're here for him, because you love him. You've always loved him, you'll always love him.

"I carry your heart in my heart," you say.

It's all you can think of to say.

Everything else has already been said.

# 31.

You are at the dance.

There is a banner on the wall that says, The Great 1980s Dance-Off.

Nothing is a surprise anymore.

You knew the banner would be there because you drew it there. It's only possible to ignore an obvious truth for so long before you have to acknowledge it.

You drew this.

You made it up.

All of it.

*"Well, it's about time. I was about to give up on you, except obviously I would never give up on you, because I love you, Nerdball. I love you forever. I'm happy for all of it, all of it, all of it. Except the end, obvs. It was all the best, right up until the end."*

"It's the end?"

*"It's the end, but you're still there. So be there for as long as you can."*

You can hear the click of your heels on the gym floor; you can feel the confetti that is falling in your teased hair—even the wig that Josh Harris is wearing is covered with it, like snow. The wig keeps slipping sideways on his smooth head, freshly shaved. You reach out and touch it. His head is so smooth. Everything about Josh Harris is everything you ever wanted it to be. You lean in and take a deep breath. The fabric of his tux is scratchy but underneath the smell of slightly-melted-from-the-iron polyester, he's still the same, toast and soap and maybe a little sweat.

"Are you wiping your nose on my jacket?" he says, and he is as real as anything has ever been. You look into his eyes and you try to laugh because, after all, Josh Harris doesn't make that many jokes, but what comes out is something different, closer to a cough. *Ribbit, ribbit.*

"I didn't like the frogs' legs," you say, because it doesn't matter that it's out of context and it doesn't make sense.

Josh Harris smiles at you and reaches out and tucks your hair behind your ear, except there is so much hair spray in there that his hand gets stuck.

"Ouch!" you say, and pull away, and you can't figure it out, after all, why it hurts when he pulls your hair, why any of this feels so real.

"It is real," says Josh Harris. "You're a good person."

You want to tell him that he's wrong, because Benedict Cumberbatch, but you don't because you're not a bad person.

You're not.

The music coming out of the speakers is tinny and scratchy, like it's time traveled here, too, from the 1980s and the lights are too bright, shining in your eyes and flashing. In the middle of the gym, a huge disco ball turns slowly and the way the light bounces off it, it looks like snow falling, a flurry of light that is falling all around you. When you half-close your good eye, the room darkens and the freckles of lights are stars and the stars are sliding slowly across a night sky and you gasp because you are on the floor and you don't know why.

Josh Harris reaches down and grabs your hand and pulls you to your feet.

"Not yet," he says. "First, we have to dance, Elyse. Let's make it count."

"You know?" you say.

"I know," he says. "How could I not know? The way you always looked at me. I liked the way I would always feel you looking, it was like you were always there for me, cheering for me, even when I didn't deserve it."

"That's a lot," you say. "That's weird, though, right?"

He shrugs. "What's *weird*? What does it matter?"

"I'm weird, I guess. I thought you thought I was pretty. Remember?"

"I think you're beautiful. I think you're perfect. I think we're perfect."

"Perfectly weird maybe."

"It's so loud, I can't really hear you."

"What?" you say. "I can't hear you! What?"

Because he's right.

It is so loud.

Everything is so loud.

The music is so loud it doesn't even sound like music, it's too loud, it's hurting your ears and you want to claw at them but Josh Harris pulls you closer and the two of you start doing a complicated dance that you never learned, but your body seems to know automatically, like something in a dream. The sound is so huge and vast and all around you, it feels like it's inside you, like it's taken over your cells and you're trying to enjoy the movement and the dance and Josh Harris but the loudness of the song is demanding something of you.

"I don't know what you want," you say. You're crying. Well, of course you're crying. "I don't know what to do."

*"I know, it's so loud, right? It's too loud. This is literally the loudest thing that's ever happened to us. You didn't draw the sound of it. You didn't draw that."*

You look up and there, hanging from the ceiling, are umbrellas. Dozens of them. Hundreds. All different colors, strung up—open—over the gym ceiling. It looks so beautiful that you stop moving and then suddenly it's quiet, there is no sound at all, only the soft smooth ink scritching softly across the slightly bumpy sketchpad.

*"That sounds like a tongue twister. Smooth ink scritching softly across the slightly bumpy sketchpad. I like it."*

The vertigo pushes you sideways and upside down. It's fine. You know you won't fall. You let Josh Harris pick you up and twirl you and spin you. You can't hear anything anymore. It's like flying. It's like how it must be for a bird soaring without flapping in the sky, carried on the back of the wind, so far above sound, so high up that there is nothing but the wind.

And now you are a bird looking down at the glorious gold red brown leaves of the fall trees and you are soaring and you are being carried and you are free and you are spinning and spinning and spinning.

No, you are *rolling*.

Down a hill, dizzy, as fast as you can.

You must do it. You have to get away.

*Escape, escape, escape.*

Nothing hurts.

Everything hurts.

The music swells again: Violin bows screech smoothly on strings. It's not nails on a chalkboard, it's something else.

*Birds*, you think. *It's birds.* All the birds, all the songs, all the sounds that have ever been played, and it doesn't hurt because it is everything.

All around you, people—the extras in the scene that you drew—are clapping, applauding, smiling for you and Josh Harris.

Of course they are: You are beautiful.

Who wouldn't clap?

They would clap, even if they *were* real. You know they would.

People would have loved to see this.

Everyone loves love.

"I love you," you say to Josh Harris.

Josh Harris pulls you close and then spins you away. Pulls you close and spins you away. And it must be happening because you can smell him, the breadiness of him, you can feel the smoothness of his skin, the firmness of his muscles. The way he grips your arm is the only thing that hurts.

The song is slowly winding down. You twirl toward him. "I know how you feel about Benedict Cumberbatch," he whispers in your ear. "Everyone gets one pass. I'll decide who mine is later and then I'll tell you."

"Maybe Emma Watson?" you say. "She seems like your type."

"Hermione?"

"Yes. She's smart. You like smart girls. Or you seem like you would. She's smarter than me."

"She's not good enough for me. She's not you. She's a zero on the scale of one to Schmidt."

"Elyse," you say. "Please. Call me Elyse."

"I can't hear you," he says. "It's so loud." He's shouting now and you can't hear him and then his face is in front of yours but his eyes are closed and you're so close to him, you can see his pores. So close.

*"Kiss him, you fool,"* says Kath, and so you think about it, but you don't do it. He's sleeping.

Josh Harris is asleep.

Your hand is on his leg. What are you doing? You snatch it back. You can't just touch him. People don't like to just be *touched.*

You don't. Although maybe you'd make an exception for Josh Harris, if he ever touched you of his own volition. *His hand on your head in the elevator, resting there.* You are desperate to talk to Kath about that, about the *pat.* The pat seemed to have more to it than just being a resting spot. The pat seemed to have meaning. A meaningful touch. You're almost sure that it meant something to him, too.

It had to.

The plane sounds noisier than it did on the way over, but no one else seems concerned. The good news is that Kath *is* talking to you and when she is talking to you that means she is about to forgive you or ask you to forgive her. She holds up a napkin and on it she's written, "Say this ten times fast: She softly slurred a slurry of sorries."

"She softly slurred a slurry of sorries," you say, dutifully. "It's fun to say out loud," you add, too softly for her to hear over the sound of the engines, and besides, she's wearing headphones.

You've forgotten who is mad at who and who needs to apologize and that's fine, because life is too short for this kind of silliness. "Sorry," you say more loudly, but you know she can't hear you. The napkin disappears. Maybe it's not important that she hears it. Maybe it's just important that you say it.

Or maybe what's important is that she's dancing and Josh Harris is asleep, next to you on a plane and the plane is beginning to vibrate and you—only you—know how this is going to go. You want to stand up and scream out a warning but who would believe you? You reach up and touch your eye, which is an eye, and something in your heart tears open, that's how much it hurts. Your eye is an eye.

Nothing happened, yet everything happened.

*No wonder Mom was so sad*, you think.

You close your eyes. "I carry your heart in my heart, too," you whisper.

You should have gone to the barn to find your dad, to tell him goodbye.

The complicating factor is that the barn doesn't exist.

There is no Schmidt's Creek.

No red truck. No Midnight. No feedstore. No lake.

There is only this: a plane, suddenly veering off course, the engine screaming in protest.

No one else has noticed yet.

How do they not notice?

"It is what it is," you say. But the thing is, it is also what it isn't.

You open the sketchpad and draw a barn quickly. So quickly, like your hand is possessed. You're shaking. "We're all going to die!" you want to shout, but maybe not. Maybe it's a mistake. A bad dream. A panic attack. You want there to be room to be wrong.

You wallow around in the tiny shred of doubt that you are allowing yourself.

You draw the sign that your dad made: SCHMIDT'S CREEK. You hang it at the bottom of the driveway of the house that doesn't exist.

You'll miss it.

You'll miss Midnight.

You'll miss Rumpelstiltskin.

You'll miss the red truck that you never drove.

You'll miss Benedict Cumberbatch.

You'll miss the silky feel of your pen against paper.

This is not a panic attack.

This is how it's going to end.

# 32.

You are on a plane.

The plane is an Airbus. It is nothing like what you would have imagined an Airbus to look like, which would have been more like an actual school bus with wings. On the seatback in front of you, a dot blinks your location over France. California is just too far away.

You change the screen. Benedict Cumberbatch smiles and turns away. "I'll be seeing you," he says. A white horse gallops by and he whistles, the horse stops in his tracks, the wind lifting his mane away from his beautiful neck. Behind the horse, the blue-green of a lake sparkles in the afternoon sun. "I'm seven percent in love with you," the actor says.

Your heart is a bird in your throat, flapping loudly in the leaves, showering you with the colors of fall in Wyoming: gold and orange and brown and green.

This is happening.

This is real.

*Pay attention*, you think.

Kath pokes her head over the back of the seat and the girl in the seat in front of her stands up and whirls around. "For God's sake, stop kicking my seat. Are you a toddler?"

"Poppy?" you say. You're standing up. You're shouting. "What are you doing here? Is this what you survived?"

"I'm afraid you've got me mixed up with someone else, and/or you're mad. Which is probable, considering the people on this plane. But your friend here has been ruining any possibility of me getting any rest on this interminable flight. I've told her ten times to stop."

"I can't control her," you point out. "I'm not her mother."

"Well, PITH YOU, Elyse Schmidt," Kath says.

"It's all happening," you say. "It's all happening. How do I stop it?" You sit down. "I don't know what to do." You turn to Josh Harris. "WAKE UP," you shout, but he doesn't.

You lean back in your seat, touching the hole in the window with your finger. Pressing on it so hard that your finger turns white.

Kath kneels up on her chair. Her face peers over the seat-back at you. Her hair is swaying, as though she's dancing, which she isn't.

"Don't say it," you say, frantically. "Please don't say it."

"You know, I was thinking—"

And then SUDDENLY she disappears.

"Kath," you say, helplessly. "There was nothing I could do." You squeeze your eyes shut and then open them again.

Why didn't you tell her to put on her seat belt?

Poppy-who-is-not-called-Poppy flies upward and her skull splits against the roof of the plane, blood is everywhere. She is dead. The first of all of you to go.

*So why was she in Survivors' Group?* You don't know what it means, you can't, because it hasn't happened and now it won't.

You dry heave into your yellow mask, which is on your face, having dropped down from the ceiling. You take it off. You don't know what to do. Josh Harris is looking at you. You put the mask back on.

He pulls his mask off. "I do not fear death," he says.

"Yes, you do. We all do, Josh," you say. "Please just say my name."

"I do not fear death," he says again. People are screaming. The swell of noise is out-of-tune violins threatening to deafen you, the desperate whine of the engines, the screams of those who are about to die. They know it. They shouldn't know but they *know*. You don't want to look, you can't look, but you look. The mom is holding her baby, her head bowed, her nose pressed to the baby's skull. She is rocking slightly, her eyes closed. You feel worse about the baby than anyone else.

The beverage cart is racing down the aisle, untended by the beautiful stewardess whose shirt was unbuttoned one row too many—the Survivors' Group leader—who has disappeared out a cavernous hole in the side of the plane where the wing used to be. People are *gone*. The air whips through the cabin, pulling and pushing at clothes and hair and tearing whole seats away. The screams, God, the screams.

"Stop screaming," you want to tell them. "Let's go gently into this good night." It doesn't make sense. This is not good. It is not night.

You would choose to live, if you *could*.

Screaming isn't choosing. The noise is unbearable.

"Shhhhh," you say, pointlessly. "Shhhhh."

You know that it's all going to take a long time from now, the stretching taffy of time means this second is forever.

"I love you," you say to Josh Harris, after taking off your mask. What does it matter? "I always loved you. I will love you forever."

"Elyse Schmidt," he says. "What is happening?"

"Just kiss me. Please call me Elyse."

"We're going to die! We're crashing! The plane is crashing!" His voice is high with hysteria. His hand is gripping your arm too tightly. He thinks you don't understand but he's wrong, you understand everything.

*Umbrellas*, you think. *Conundrum*.

Then it is just you and Josh Harris, alone, acting out this scene.

"I'm sorry I didn't know you, Elyse," he shouts, and then he kisses you. It's hard because gravity has run amok. Arms, legs, everywhere. So much noise. The noise is terrible. The noise is tearing you apart.

The screen with Benedict Cumberbatch's face on it is frozen, then it flickers and shuts off. The novel that Josh

Harris had been reading flies out of the seat pocket in front of him and lands on you. *Wa a Pea*, says the torn cover.

"I'm pretty sure there *is* peace at the end," you try to say, when before you are quite ready for it, you really aren't ready yet, the mountain rushes up and crashes into you with such unbelievable force that you can feel all your molecules tearing apart, one from another, and you wish you couldn't feel it because the pain is unbearable and also familiar.

Your mouth is full of blood and teeth and regret for all the things you didn't do and you are crying for the year when you were seventeen, which isn't going to happen.

Things like this are not survivable.

The thing is that there isn't a choice, there isn't *always* a choice, sometimes the choice is made for you, and you're left in that split second between dead and alive and that part can be filled in with a whole life of lakes and lightning, of kissing and falling stars. Just a splice in time when all of the everything can happen that will ever happen and now you can just stop trying so hard, you can just let go.

It's okay.

You have to.

Just *release*.

You unbuckle and fall forward, blood in your mouth, blood in your eye, so much blood, hitting the ground hard, your bones crumpling on impact, but you roll anyway. It feels necessary to do this part, this effort of rolling, it's important. The mountainside is steep and covered with gravel and ice and bits of grass and somehow, impossibly, wildflowers that you can smell, a tangy overpowering scent.

The light is everywhere.

The light is all around you, over and under you, and you keep rolling in slow motion because you know this is how it goes, this is what you are meant to do.

And then there is the smell of the jet fuel closing up your nose and mouth and throat and you are suffocating and a tiny purple flower, perfectly encased in ice, is right in your sight line. You could stop rolling and you could just look at it, see how perfect it is, each tiny petal, but blood has run into your eyes and everything is hazy and blurry and you have to keep rolling.

Then there is the explosion you knew was coming and the ball of light and heat and the thrust that pushes you into the ravine, and the *searing* and you're falling now and you land on a body, which you know is Josh Harris.

He is breathing.

"Elyse," he says.

"I am the leaf," you say. "I'm sorry."

The leaf is dark green, pink-veined, crumpling and tearing into a million pieces, but safe for cats and dogs.

And then there is the inferno of heat that tastes like fuel and life and death and it is strangling you.

The heat is too much, you are both curling up—you and Josh Harris and what you could have had together—around the edges like paper in a flame, blackening and vanishing into ash and you can feel it, you shouldn't be able to feel it, but you can and this is what it is, this is death, and this is you and Josh Harris and Kath, and the girl who is not Poppy and the Other Max and the Right Max and Danika Prefontaine and

Charlie Martin and the baby and Mr. Appleby and the flight attendant and all of you are *light*, it's amazing that all this white light has come from all that black destruction, ash, and flame. Two hundred and eighteen bolts of lightning all moving in reverse, up toward the sky, not away. It is happening to everyone from your class and it is happening to the other passengers on the plane and it is happening to Josh Harris and it is happening to you. You suppose that by the time the rescuers come, all of your light will have vanished up behind the curtain of night.

No one will see this.

No one will understand how you are the light, the lightning, the rain, the stars; how you are love and umbrellas and conundrums.

And now you are the everything, all of you, not *just* you and Josh Harris anymore, but everyone, and there is no more sound and nothing hurts and no one is screaming and you are the trees and you are the golden leaves and you are the birds and the peaches and the music and the red truck with the keys tucked up in the visor and the coyote's howl and the dog barking at the siren in the night and the white horse tossing his mane and galloping across a field of wildflowers somewhere in a state you've never known, where you'll never be, that you carry in your heart, in a small suitcase: What could have been, what isn't, what wasn't, and what will never be.

# Acknowledgments

To the amazing team of people at Algonquin, who feel more like a family, and who continue to support me even when I say, "But what if I write this one in the second person?"—thank you.

To my agent, Jennifer Laughran, who has never once confirmed my secret fears, even when I present a very convincing argument—thank you.

To my mum, who has supported me forever, and who listens when I say, "I don't think I can do it!" and gently corrects me. I love you. And thank you.

To my dad, who is always my first and most supportive reader. Thank you for always saying the right thing. I love you.

To my local friends, who seem okay with the fact that I drop out of sight for months at a time, only to emerge when they are just starting to forget who I am—thank you.

To my faraway friends, who, via the internet, have saved me over and over and over again—thank you.

To all the writers whose books I read and love and learn from and fall asleep with every night—thank you.

To the plane crash survivor who, in a news interview, said, "It looked like the mountain was coming toward us. It took me a second to figure out what was actually happening." That description stuck with me and spawned this story. Thank you.

To Uma, who walks with me and listens to all my crazy ideas unspooling in the woods and reminds me what's important—thank you.

To the gatekeepers, who understand that while one book is rarely right for *everybody*, all books are right for at least one *somebody*—thank you.

And to my kids, who sometimes forget how deadlines turn our lives upside down in fits and starts, you'll both have my heart always and forever.

And of course, to the readers, who see what they need to see in the words I've written. It's all for you. ♥ Thank you. Thank you. Thank you.

I'm so grateful.